CRASHING DOWN

CATHRYN FOX

For Cher Kilgore
Thanks for all you do for me. You're a gem and I
appreciate you so much!

CHAPTER ONE

"You reek of sex."

Noah Ryan grinned at his buddy Jared, a guy he'd gotten to know over the last couple of years while living and working at Stone Cliff Resort in the Canadian Rocky Mountains. Taking his friend's ribbing in stride, Noah scrubbed his hands through his disheveled hair, and sank down onto the driftwood next to him, setting his motorcycle helmet at his feet. He let his glance surf over the crowd gathered around the nightly, beachside bonfire. He zeroed in on a cute blonde with big tits and gave Jared a wry smirk. "Not yet I don't."

Jared reached into the cooler, pulled out a cold brew, and handed it to Noah. "Yeah, well that's a matter of opinion."

"Fuck you." Noah laughed and twisted off the cap, the taste of weed and smoke scratching his dry throat like coarse sandpaper. "How the hell can I reek of sex when I just crawled out of bed, *alone*?"

Jared shrugged. "Well your bed smells like sex, then."

Okay, so that was probably true. His bed likely did

smell like sex. Sometimes a hard, mindless fuck chased away the chills that had taken up residency inside him since the accident a little over three years ago. Then again, sometimes it didn't. Sometimes the demons managed to tunnel their way past the wall he'd built despite a warm body lying next to him.

Noah took a long pull from the bottle, and washed the grit from his throat. Too bad the alcohol did little to drown the pain that blackened his soul. Then again, did he really deserve for it to?

He worked to push all dark thoughts aside, and tried to keep things light. He nudged his friend with his elbow. "Ah, come on, Jared. Don't be jealous 'cause I'm getting all the play and you're not."

Jared waved to Ryan and Bobbie, a couple of locals who had just rolled in, before he flicked his beer cap at Noah. "Yeah, well, fuck you. I get all the play I need, or I would be if you weren't always hovering around." Two well-built, dark-haired hotties moved in front of them, smiling flirtatiously at Noah. "Christ, Noah, what the hell is it about you?" He clucked his tongue and added, "You're like nectar to the honey bee, my man."

Laughing, Noah took another swig from the bottle as the cute blonde he'd been eying glanced his way. He caught the mischief in her gaze and pegged her as a local, a rich townie who'd just returned home from university. He knew her type all too well. She'd spend her days lounging on the water with her friends and her nights here at the beach, otherwise known as the Cave, where many of the resort staff and locals alike gathered for a little action. Not that he was judging her. He wasn't. After all, unlike him she was getting an education and going places.

With exhaustion pulling at him, Noah stretched his arms over his head and stifled a yawn. He hadn't planned on hanging out with Jared tonight, but since he couldn't take staring at his ceiling for one more minute, he'd decided if he couldn't sleep, he might as well get laid. The little townie gave him a look that said, *come get some* and his cock twitched, but before he made his move on the blonde, he shifted closer to his friend. He pulled an envelope from his back pocket and slipped it to him, wanting to do this exchange off resort and away from their manager, Donald Brake's, watchful eye.

"Noah..." Jared looked down at the envelope and shook his head. "Shit." He stole a quick glance around before he shoved the bills into his pocket. "But you were saving...you can't afford—"

"And you can't afford not to." He looked pointedly at the swelling beneath Jared's bruised eye. Even though he claimed the injury had happened when he fell off the raft during yesterday's rough, white-water ride down Canyon Run, Noah knew better. Noah pitched his voice low, his words for Jared's ears only. "You keep fucking with these guys and you'll lose more than just your job. You know that, right?"

"Yeah, yeah, I know," Jared said gravely, dark eyes cast downward in worry as he rubbed his temples with his thumbs. "Christ, I had a straight flush. I never thought I could lose." He fisted his short-cropped hair and gave a tug. "I mean come on, what are the fucking odds that the other guy beat me with a royal flush?"

"A trillion to one," Noah said. He didn't need to do the mental math that came so easily to him as he finished off his beer and reached for another, handing one to Jared as well. Even though Jared was as big a fuck up as he was, the guy was a damn hard worker, and in a few short years had climbed his way up from bellboy to concierge. That job was his life, and Noah wasn't about to stand around and see it get taken from him.

It was Jared's job to get to know the guests and see that their needs were being met. What he wasn't supposed to do was socialize with those guests, or get himself invited to the after-hours poker game that the resort's management turned a blind eye to. The high-rolling businessmen, who came to town for the annual weeklong event, weren't the kind of guys who took kindly to getting stiffed. You owed them money, you paid your debt. One way or another.

Noah's glance shot to the blonde. Then again, who was he too lecture about rules, considering he was about to break one himself? Even when off duty, the staff wasn't supposed to do anything to bring negative attention to the resort, which meant that picking up a local for a quick fuck on the rocks was pretty much all kinds of wrong.

"I'll pay you back," Jared said.

The blonde gave Noah a once over and a satisfied grin. "You just keep yourself out of trouble."

Jared followed the direction of Noah's gaze, and when he glimpsed the girl Noah had his sights set on, he shook his head. "You're one to talk. That girl has trouble written all over her."

"Good," Noah said, smirking.

"She's got a boyfriend, Noah," Jared warned. "And he's a big bastard."

"I think you're mistaken." Ignoring Jared's warning, Noah stood and shoved one hand into his pocket, pulling his worn and faded jeans lower on his hips, a not so subtle invitation that brought the blonde's attention right where he wanted it. "I think she's looking for a little play."

Jared gave him a look that suggested he was either crazy, or had a death wish, or possibly both. Maybe he was right.

"Yeah? What makes you say that?" Jared asked.

"She wouldn't be wearing a shirt that showed off her tits if she didn't want me to look."

While Jared cursed under his breath, Noah moved through the throng of people. Seconds before he reached blondie, some douche bag stepped in front of him to block his path. Noah nudged him with his shoulder, shoving him out of the way. With single-minded determination he moved past him, but when the guy said, "Is there a problem here, pal?" it stopped Noah dead in his tracks.

He turned and sized up the steroid-induced mouth breather and shrugged. "Listen dude," Noah began. "As far as I can tell the only problem here is that you're standing between me," he paused to poke his finger in the direction of the girl watching him with big, curious eyes, "and her."

The guy grabbed Noah's arm, his nostrils flaring as he yanked Noah closer. Even at six feet, Noah had to lift his chin to meet the guy's eyes. The ogre gripped him tighter, his sausage fingers digging into Noah's biceps.

Like a wire stretched tight, Noah snapped. "Get the fuck off me." His skin came alive as he jerked his arm free. Christ, he didn't like to be touched. Touching made him feel...well, it made him *feel*.

Old, blood-soaked memories clawed their way to the surface, and visions of his best friend clutching his arm like it was his lifeline swamped him. But Noah hadn't been Jonny's lifeline. Oh no, not at all. Noah was a fuck up, and the sole reason Jonny was dead.

"...Noah."

He heard Jared saying something, pleading with him, but the words were lost in the foggy haze clouding his mind, riding circles around his brain on the pain that came with remembering.

"Maybe you should listen to your boyfriend," the ogre said.

Noah laughed in his face. "Maybe you should suck my dick."

The mouth breather fisted his hands and drew his arm back. Heart racing, Noah stood there, his body braced as he prepared for the pain. Welcomed it.

Deserved it.

Like a hard fuck, sometimes a good punch in the face sent the demons scurrying. For a little while, anyway.

The hit came sure and swift, and Noah's teeth clashed as he flew backwards toward the water. The damp sandy shore padded his fall, but the cold waves crashing over his body snapped his groggy senses back to life faster than a broken condom. He jumped to his feet and spit a mouth full of blood onto the sand as the primate came at him again, his knuckles practically dragging on the ground.

"Stop it, Alex," a shrill voice cried out, and Noah's heart sank as the girl he'd been stalking halted the fight. Jesus, he'd wanted that next blow. Craved it. Noah wiped his mouth with the back of his hand as blondie pounded her fists into Alex's chest.

Fuck if Jared hadn't been right. Blondie did have a boyfriend, and the big bastard's name was Alex.

Alex grabbed the girl's hands, and pinned them to her sides. She squirmed and fought against him, the back of her shirt lifting to show a tramp stamp that Noah was certain her good folks knew nothing about. Damned if she wasn't just the girl he needed tonight.

"Stay out of this, Dara," the ape named Alex warned.

Noah took a threatening step toward Alex. "Take your fucking hands off her."

"Noah," Jared warned again as the crowd gathered around them. The bonfire burned bright, the fiery embers sparking like angry fireflies in the dark night sky, casting a flickering spotlight on the scene playing out before them. "You start this shit again, and Donald won't give you any more chances," he bit out harshly, but Noah was too far gone, too far down the road filled with blood and bad memories to walk away.

"I didn't start it." He swiped his tongue over his swollen lip and jutted his chin toward Alex. "He did. I'm just going to finish it." Noah stood there, sizing up his opponent once again, waiting for him to make another move.

Alex looked at Noah, then at his girlfriend, who continued to struggle against his grip. Suspicion moved into his beady eyes as they locked on hers. "What are you protecting this guy for? Do you know him or something?" he asked, his voice slurring slightly.

"We're all just here to have a good time, Alex."

"A good time?" He jerked his head toward Noah, his lips curling with disgust. "That's the good time you want?" Silence hung heavy for a moment, then sweet tits shrugged, everything in what she didn't say answering Alex's question. "This shit ain't worth it." He shoved Dara away, pushed through the crowd and stormed down the beach.

He watched Alex disappear and then turned his attention to Dara. "You okay?"

Big eyes moved over his swollen lip as her two friends came up behind her. "Are you?" she asked.

Noah scrubbed his hand over his jaw. "Your boyfriend throws one hell of a punch."

She took a sip from the cooler her friend handed her, looking at him over the rim of the bottle. She swallowed and licked her lips before saying, "Maybe he's not my boyfriend anymore."

"Is that right?" Noah asked, inching closer and invading her personal space. Damn she smelled good.

"Well, maybe not tonight, anyway." She nibbled her bottom lip, a seductive move Noah figured she'd perfected in front of a mirror, and then slid her gaze over his body.

"You gotta be fucking kidding me." The sound of

Jared's voice from behind him pulled Noah's attention away from those luscious lips.

Noah cast him a quick glance and smirked. "What?"

"Like you even have to ask." Shaking his head, Jared disappeared into the crowd, leaving Noah to do what he did best. Fuck everything up.

With the fight over, the crowd went back to partying, and Dara stepped in and closed the small space that remained between them. She went up on her tiptoes, those nice tits of hers pressing into his chest. Reaching up, she feathered her fingertip over his swollen lip. "Does it hurt?"

"Yeah. It hurts like a son of a bitch. But I guess that's to be expected when I use my face to stop a punch."

She puckered those pouty lips of hers and all Noah could think about was how that sexy mouth would feel around his cock.

"You think I should kiss it better?"

Noah grinned. Christ, she made this so easy. "I think that's a good start."

She handed her cooler back to her friends, and gave the cute brunette a knowing smile before she turned back to Noah. With a tip of her head, she gestured behind her. "Maybe we should...you know...go somewhere private."

She didn't need to ask him twice. Noah grabbed her hand and pulled her away from the crowd. Once they were out of sight, near the rocky cliff at the far end of the beach, he stepped into the water and splashed a palm full into his mouth. He sloshed it around to wash away the blood, and then spat it out.

Not wasting any time, he gripped Dara's hips, his cock swelling inside his jeans as he pushed her up against the rock wall. He dipped his head, his lips so close to hers that he could taste the raspberry cooler on her breath. Goddamn she had a mouth made for sucking. He slipped one hand around the back of her neck, the floral scent of her hair filling his nostrils as his eyes latched on her hot mouth.

"So about that kiss," he murmured.

Her tongue flicked out to moisten her bottom lip and ignoring the split on his lip, he crushed his mouth to hers. The pressure stung like a bitch, but he didn't care. He groaned as sensations overcame him, let them push back the memories that came far too close to the surface tonight. His tongue slipped inside to thrash with hers as his hands went to her tits. He palmed them and she moaned, wiggling against him. With his mouth watering for a taste of her nipples, he gripped the hem of her shirt and tugged.

He pulled it over her head and inched back to look at her lace bra. "Sweet," he murmured and she smiled at him, the look on her face telling him she knew she was as sexy as hell and could have whoever she wanted. He was fine with that. She wanted a good time, and tonight he was the guy she'd chosen to provide it. It wasn't his fault she picked a no good loser like him. But some of the townies liked to go slumming during their summer break, and as long as he was getting a piece of ass, he was cool with it.

He reached behind her back, made quick work of the metal hook, and then tossed the bra onto the rocks along with her shirt. Pushing a knee between her legs, he widened them and bent to draw a hard nipple into his mouth.

Her hands raked through his hair and she whimpered. He ignored the pain in his jaw and sucked deep, needing to get lost in her. Her hands moved to his shirt, and she tugged at the material. He reached behind his neck and tugged it over his shoulders, adding it to the pile forming on the rocks. Once he was half naked, she raced those soft fingers over him.

"Nice tat," she whispered, tracing the cross

tombstone on his arm.

An uneasy tremble moved through him as she stroked him. He grabbed her hands, put them behind her and lightly brushed the tattoo at the small of her back. "I like yours, too."

She made a move to reach for him again, but he pushed against her, caging her hands between her ass and the rock. "Keep them there," he ordered.

She looked like she was going to protest, but when he released the button on her shorts, and shoved his hand inside, a low moan rose from her throat. His cock throbbed against her thigh and she sucked in a quick breath when he dipped inside her panties to finger her pussy. A whimpering sound bubbled up from her throat.

"Feel good, baby?" he asked.

"So good," she said, bucking against his hand.

He pushed a finger inside her and his mind shut down when he felt her wetness. "Jesus, you're drenched," he growled. He pushed deep, and while she looked so fucking hot in her short shorts, with his hand inside her panties, he couldn't get a good finger bang going with her still dressed.

Panting hard, and keeping a finger inside her, he said, "Take your shorts off."

She pulled her hands out from behind her, pushed her shorts down and wiggled them to her feet. Her pussy tightened around his finger with her movements. With his free hand, Noah pulled them from her ankles and tossed them onto the pile.

Leaning up against the rocks, she spread her legs wide to give him better access, and the sweet scent of her hot pussy hit him like a double shot of rum. The world around him faded, dulled to a hush. He pushed his finger in and out of her, until she was so soaked and ready that all he could think about was ramming his dick into her.

Her hands went to his zipper. "Take yours off too," she said breathlessly. "I want to see your cock."

Noah groaned. Oh yeah, this girl really was all kinds of trouble.

He pulled his finger out of her pussy, tore off his pants, and threw them on top of her clothes. His cock jutted forward, so hard and ready his brain was nearly blank. Jesus, he loved it when his brain shut down. Her gaze dropped, and she made a whimpering sound as she reached for his dick. He nudged his hips forward, offering it to her. It was true he didn't like to be touched, but when a chick wanted to stroke his dick, he damn well made an exception.

"So big," she murmured.

"You like it big, baby?"

"Yeah." She licked her mouth, her hands grasping his cock harder.

Noah swallowed hard. "You want to suck it?"

She gave him a sexy grin that told him how much she liked sucking cock, how good she was at it, before she sank to her knees. The second her mouth wrapped around his crown, he gripped her head with one hand and braced the other on the rock wall behind her. Christ, her hot wet mouth felt so damn good.

"Fuck..."

She moaned around a mouthful of cock, and he rocked into her, hitting the back of her throat. She gagged a little, but continued to try to take him deeper.

"Nice," he murmured, ramming into her.

She licked the long length of him, her tongue running circles around his crown before she plunged forward to take him back in again. She spent a long time working him in and out of her hot mouth, and when he groaned, she cupped his balls. They drew up tight against his body, and knowing he was close to coming in her mouth, he inched back, and hauled her against him, desperate to bury himself inside her.

He gripped her hips, and lifted her until she was sitting on the ledge, shoving his shirt underneath her ass. His fingers bit into her thighs as he widened them. Bending forward to better position himself between her spread legs, he swiped her cunt with his tongue, and she jutted her tits forward as she leaned back, her palms braced on the rock behind her.

Noah grabbed his pants, and pulled a condom from the pocket. He tore into it and rolled the rubber down the long length of cock.

Dara's eyes widened in anticipation as he wrapped one arm around her slim waist for leverage, and positioned his cock at her entrance.

"You ready to fuck?" he asked.

Instead of answering she wiggled her hips, forcing him in an inch.

"Christ," he groaned as her heat wrapped around him. He held her tighter, and in one quick thrust powered into her. She gasped and rubbed her hard nipples against his chest.

He pumped deep, fast, ramming so hard he was sure they were going to punch through the rock wall. She moved with him, and he inched back to look between their bodies as he pulled out, only to sink all the way back inside again. Jesus, she was hot...

He fucked her long and hard, until her body tightened and she made a whimpering sound. A second later her hot cream singed his cock. As her muscles squeezed his dick, she reached for him again, but he pinned her arms to her sides and pumped feverishly. He knew he was being rough, knew he was going to leave her bruised come morning, but there was nothing he could do to slow down. He needed to fuck. He needed to forget. Oh, God, he just needed...

His cock swelled to the point of no return, every

nerve in his body alive and on fire. He drove all the way insider her, burying himself balls deep as he let go, splashing his seed into the condom. He threw his head back and growled, concentrating on the explosions rocketing through him. She squeezed him with her cunt, milking every last drop of his release.

Sweat trickled down his brow, and he swiped it away as he strived to catch his breath. Dara shifted and pulled away, his cock slipping out of her. He stood back, water splashing against his heels as he disposed of the rubber. Dara reached for her clothes and pulled them on quickly. Once she was dressed, she jumped from the ledge and grinned up at him.

"Thanks," she said, licking her lips and smoothing down her long blonde hair as her skin glistened with perspiration. "That was fun."

"Yeah," he said, his voice rough, edgy as he reached behind her to grab his pants. She stepped around him, and he said, "I'll guess I'll see you around." He tugged his jeans on and gave a casual roll of his shoulder.

"Sure. I'll be around," she said and then disappeared down the beach, dismissing him like he was nothing but a go nowhere loser, a go-to guy when a girl needed to scratch an itch.

What bothered him the most was that she was right.

CHAPTER TWO

Keeping her head high and back straight, Kathryn Lane lowered herself into the chair opposite her new boss at Stone Cliff Resort in the heart of Alberta's Rocky Mountains. She crossed her legs at the ankles, and poised her tablet on her lap, ready to dive into her new position as Marketing Assistant.

"Kathryn," her boss Shannon began, flashing her a warm, welcoming smile, but behind that smile Kathryn could easily tell she was a serious businesswoman, one who didn't tolerate anything but perfection. "I see personnel placed you in Wolf Lodge. Are you all settled in for the summer?"

Kathryn nodded, thinking about the small room that resembled her dorm at Sanford, Canada's prestigious, East Coast University where she had just finished her junior year. At least at the resort her room had a private shower and the staff quarters had a small, communal kitchen so she didn't have to eat mystery meat in the meal hall every day. And when she didn't feel like cooking for herself, she could use one of her staff meal tickets to dine on low fat, healthy food at the buffet.

"Yes, thank you," she responded, keeping an air of professionalism about her.

Shannon looked at her over her dark-rimmed glasses. "You know this week is all about settling in. You didn't have to come in until Monday."

"I wanted to get an early start."

"Very well." Shannon's silver hair glistened in the sunlight shining in from her window as she pulled open a file with Kathryn's name on it. She adjusted her glasses lower on her nose, and went quiet for a moment as she read. "So you're internship is for the full four months?"

"Yes," Kathryn answered. "It's part of my scholarship requirement."

Shannon slipped a paper from the file and her perfectly sculpted brows went up as she looked it over. "I'm impressed. It's not every day we get a scholar like you interning for us. I expect great things."

Kathryn smiled her usual smile, never hinting at what she'd had to give up in order to get where she was. No friends. No dates. No dreams. Her father would have none of that. No, his only daughter had to work, work, work, and stand above the rest.

"Thank you. I'm looking forward to getting started," she said cheerily, even though inside she was tied up in knots. While she'd worked hard and was extremely grateful that she had won one of Canada's largest university scholarships, the pressures that came with it could sometimes be overwhelming. Not only did she have to maintain an exceptionally high average in all her classes, she had to perform well during her summer break internships, which challenged her in three disciplines: enterprise, public policy, and community development. Combining those pressures with a president and CEO father who was always breathing down her back, pushing her to do better than her best, so she could graduate at the top of her class and secure herself a corner office in his financial consulting firm, certainly made for challenging times.

Shannon handed her a pile of brochures, and a thick book on the resort that contained the mission statement and marketing plans. "You can look these over on the weekend," she said.

Kathryn nodded, and Shannon opened her mouth to say something else, but closed it again when a noise outside her office door drew her attention. Shannon looked over Kathryn's shoulders, a frown on her pretty face as she zeroed in on something or someone in the resort lobby. Curious, Kathryn angled her head to see what the commotion was all about.

She took in all the new staff who were milling about, getting themselves acquainted with the resort and settled in for the summer. She peered through the crowd, until she caught a glimpse of a guy standing outside the resort manager's door. Dressed in staff colors, his snug green t-shirt with the resort logo on it hugged his broad shoulders, and showcased a hard body. On his left arm, she caught a hint of a tattoo dipping below the short sleeve. Her gaze dropped to his low hanging swimming trunks, and the clipboard he clutched tightly in his hand. He seemed to be in deep discussions with Donald Brake, the manager with whom Kathryn had interviewed with to get the assistant's job.

Kathryn glanced at Shannon. "What's going on?"

Shannon sighed. "That's Noah. He teaches skiing in the winter and is a river guide for the white-water rafting tours at Canyon Run in the summer."

"He seems upset."

"It's nothing for you to worry about." When Kathryn nodded, accepting the answer without question, her boss leaned in like she was about to confide something personal. "You probably won't cross paths with him,

Kathryn." Shannon paused to look over Kathryn's prim, knee length pencil skirt, and chic blazer. Feeling a bit uncomfortable under her scrutiny, Kathryn smoothed her hand over her hair, checking to make sure it was still secured tightly in her ponytail. Shannon's eyes moved back to hers and she smiled. "I'm sure you won't be running in the same circles during your time here."

"Oh, okay," Kathryn said, for lack of anything else.

Shannon went quiet for a moment and then advised, "You might want to pick your friends carefully here. Relationships between staff members aren't forbidden, but they are frowned upon because they can interfere with work. I'm certain you wouldn't want to do anything to interfere with your job or your scholarship, isn't that right?"

Kathryn nodded. Point taken.

Still, unable to help herself, she stole another glance at Noah. As if he felt his eyes on her, he turned his head toward her. When their glances collided, he gifted her with a smile, a smile so hot and disarming, it sucked the breath from Kathryn's lungs. *What the heck?* She exhaled slowing, trying to appear unaffected as she turned back to Shannon, who thankfully, was looking over her file once again.

"I guess we'll get started then," Shannon said. "Since you'll be working on the brochures, the first thing I need you to do is familiarize yourself with the resort. You need to know all the ins and outs, and all the activities we offer." Shannon gestured with her hand when someone came in the door behind Kathryn.

"Amy, come in. I was just about to call for you."

Kathryn smiled at Amy as she came bouncing in, a big smile lighting up her pretty face.

"Hey there," Amy said to Kathryn as she extended her arm. They exchanged a handshake as Shannon did the introductions.

"This is Amy's third summer with us. She's a psychology student, and she works registration and sometimes helps me out," Shannon explained. "I asked her to show you around today, and I believe Amy lives at Wolf Lodge as well. Isn't that right, Amy?"

"Sure is," Amy said, her long, dark hair as bouncy and bubbly as her personality. "Are you ready?" she asked.

"Absolutely," Kathryn said, turning off her tablet and putting it in her bag.

For the next few hours Amy showed her around, and even though her personality was very different from Kathryn's, Kathryn couldn't help but like her. Amy helped to familiarize her with all the facilities, including the spa, horse stables, dining room, biking trails, ski hills, and tennis courts. Once they were done, they took the shuttle to Deerfield, the closest town.

Amy talked nonstop during the tour and as they drove past a beach area that looked like it had had a fire recently, she gave a grin. "That's the Cave. It's where we go to have a little off-resort fun." She nudged Kathryn. "If you know what I mean." She looked at Kathryn's business clothes and then at her own. "Tonight we'll get out of these work clothes and into something a little sexier."

Instead of telling her she didn't have clothes that were sexy, she just nodded and looked at the mountains in the distance. Amy pointed out the amenities, and when they drove down a side road, the brick buildings full of gorgeous graffiti, Kathryn's heart leapt, thrilled that Deerfield had an art district.

Kathryn pointed at the wall. "Who did that?"

Amy's eyes widened. "Gorgeous isn't it?"

"Yeah," Kathryn agreed, taking in the lines, shading and composition. "Whoever did that was very talented." She thought more about art, art history, and murals, her true love. A knot tightened in her throat. She swallowed it down, because she knew better than to let her thoughts travel that path. While her father collected numerous art pieces, a career in the arts, or switching to a fine arts degree certainly wasn't in the cards for his daughter.

Their last stop on the tour was the white-water rafting adventure at Canyon Run River. They arrived just in time to see one of the boats returning, the thrill-seekers inside laughing as they wrung water from their hair. They disembarked, and that's when she caught a glimpse of Noah at the back of the boat. He pulled off his helmet, and wiped the water from his face. Kathryn felt her mouth go dry.

"Looks like fun," Kathryn said, when in reality the whole idea of rushing down a river scared the hell out of her. She didn't take risks. Her every action was calculated and had a greater purpose. Of course, that didn't mean she didn't want to. Except such behavior was frowned upon in her world.

"We can sign you up for a run if you like?" Amy said.

Her glance shot to Amy, then back to Noah. If he was part of the deal, then maybe she'd give it a shot. Okay, where the heck did that crazy thought come from?

"Have you ever done it?" Kathryn asked.

Amy licked her lips and gave her a wicked grin. "Not yet, but I sure do want to."

When she caught the way Amy was drooling over Noah, Kathryn said, "Uh, wait, are we still talking about rafting?"

Amy laughed. "Nope."

Kathryn turned her attention to Noah, her glance moving over his body, which looked mighty fine in that wetsuit. They both stood there in mute silence as they watched him secure the boat on shore. He unzipped the wetsuit, pulling it from his shoulders to expose a very tight, very hard body, one with a tombstone cross with a J in the center on his left arm.

Amy groaned. "God he's so hot."

"Yes, he certainly is," Kathryn murmured, but then instantly straightened her shoulders. "I mean, yes, but he's not my type."

Amy rolled her eyes. "Come on, Kathryn, he's every girl's type."

And that was exactly why mooning over him was a waste of time. A hot guy like him would never look twice at a bookworm virgin like her. Kathryn shrugged off the comment, but try as she might, she couldn't tear her gaze away from him. It was like coming upon a bad car accident and being compelled to stop and view the wreckage.

Her gaze lingered over his split lip and then left his face to admire his abs. She suddenly wondered what it would be like to touch them.

"Time to head back," Amy said with a sigh, pulling Kathryn's thoughts back.

"Right," she said, shaking her head to clear it. Good God, what was wrong with her? She wasn't into guys like Noah. Heck, she wasn't into guys at all. She could almost hear her father's voice. *Boyfriends get in the way, relationships distract from your greater purpose.*

Even when it did come time for her to bring a member of the opposite sex home, it certainly wouldn't be someone like Noah, a boy who had trouble written all over him—one her new boss had not so subtly warned her to stay away from. Then again, she'd probably never get the chance to bring a boy home. No, her father probably already had a boring accountant from his firm picked out for her.

A boring guy to go with her boring life.

For the rest of her boring life.

Perfect, just perfect.

* * *

Noah braced his hands above the doorjamb and looked at Jared as he pushed papers across his desk. "I guess I owe you a thank you."

Jared met his glance and said, "You don't owe me anything."

"Yeah, well, Donald would have fired my sorry ass if it weren't for you."

He pointed to his eye. "And I would have been floating at the bottom of the river if it weren't for you."

Noah plunked himself down on the seat opposite Jared. "Okay, so enough of this pussy shit. Are you hitting the Cave tonight, or what?" He rubbed his hands. "It's initiating night. Time to give the summer staff a nice warm welcome to Stone Cliff."

Jared grimaced like he was reliving his own dunk in the lake. "You mean a cold welcome."

"So you're going then?"

"That depends."

"On what?"

"Are you going to be there?"

"Yeah, why?"

Instead of answering, Jared said, "Come on, let's go eat. I'm starved."

Noah's stomach growled, a reminder that he hadn't eaten since rafting down Canyon Run earlier that afternoon. He smirked and said, "Yeah, I can see how you've worked up an appetite, pushing the pile of paper around, and all."

Jared gestured toward the cut on the corner of Noah's mouth, reminding him of his fight with the Neanderthal last night. "Yeah, well, we're not all suicide junkies like you."

They walked toward the kitchen, passing by

Shannon's office. Noah glanced in, catching a glimpse of the cute red-head he'd caught staring at him earlier that morning when he was getting reamed by Donald, and again later today down at Canyon Run.

"Who's the new girl?" he asked.

"Kathryn Lane," Jared said, not bothering to look to see who Noah was talking about. That was the all-knowing, all-seeing Jared, always had his finger on the pulse of the resort. "Scholarship student. She's here for a summer internship."

An uneasy shiver moved through Noah as he gave her a once over. It wasn't the way she kept her back rigid, or the way she had her strawberry hair pulled back in a tight ponytail that had him thinking back to three years ago. It was her focus. The way she seemed to tune the whole world out as she concentrated on her task, like it was the most important thing in the entire world. Noah had learned the hard way that it wasn't.

"Forget it, Noah," Jared said.

"Forget what?" Luke asked, as he caught up with the two of them on the way to the kitchen. Noah knew Jared considered Luke a friend, but Noah, well, he'd rather run his raft into a rock wall than hang out with the guy. As far as he was concerned, Luke was a bit of a douche, always walking around like he thought he was better than everyone else. So what if he was a super star tennis player, taken out by an injury during the world's junior a few years back. Now, thanks to his family's connections, he had a nice cushy job at the resort, giving lessons—on and off the court—to some of the hottest ass around. And to top that off, he took a three-month hiatus in the summer, hanging out with his family in Europe during the resort's busiest months. What twenty-three-year-old needed a hiatus? From the second Noah stepped onto the resort, Luke had seemed to take an instant dislike to him. He'd never come out and said it to his face, but there was no denying the tension between them.

Jared jerked his head toward Shannon's office as they passed. "Noah was checking out the new girl."

"Oh yeah? Well forget it, pal," Luke sneered and ran his hand over his gelled hair. "A girl like that would never fall for your bullshit."

"It's not my bullshit they fall for," Noah said, grabbing his cock.

"You're such a crude bastard," Luke said. "Regardless, you're not her type."

"And you are?"

A sour look moved over Luke's face as he let his glance rake over Noah's work clothes. Then he waved a hand over his own body. Christ, the guy looked like a fucking pussy in his designer brand polo shirt and golf shorts. Noah could understand having to wear shit like that on the court, but the guy was off duty.

"Come on, Noah, you can't be serious," Luke said. "She's out of your league."

"Probably. But I bet I can get her to go out with me. In fact, I bet I can get her to do a lot of things with me."

"Oh really? Then I guess I'll take you up on that."

Wait! Shit, what had he just agreed to? He thought back to the pretty girl who looked like she was all work and no play. His gut tightened, because everything inside him told him that he should have kept his big mouth shut. Getting her to go out with him was a bad idea. Not because he wasn't up for the challenge, but because he saw way too much of himself in her. Too much of the guy he used to be and never wanted to be again.

"Isn't fucking around with staff forbidden?" Noah asked, hedging a direct answer.

"It's frowned upon." Luke made air quotes as they entered the kitchen area. "Not forbidden."

With a shake of his head, Jared grabbed a tray and moved ahead of them, leaving them to hash out the details of the bet Noah knew better than to accept. Then again, he was the one who had put it out there. Jesus, he was such a fuck up.

"What's good?" Jared asked the kitchen staff.

"Lasagna," the head chef, Mario said in a very thick Italian accent. He looked past Jared's shoulder and met Noah's glance. "Nice and cheesy, just the way you like it, Noah."

Working to keep things light, Noah stepped up to Mario and slapped him on the back. "You're the man." Reaching into his back pocket, Noah pulled out the two tickets a guest had given to him as a thank you for a fun time white water rafting. While he wasn't allowed to accept cash tips, sometimes the guests rewarded him with things like vouchers and tickets.

"Take the wife out to the drive-in tonight." He gave him a wink, and said, "Maybe you'll get lucky and something really boring will be playing."

Mario laughed. "You're too good to me," he said as he put an extra heaping of lasagna onto Noah's plate.

Luke, who barely spared the cook a look, took his tray and made his way toward the back room, where staff ate separately from the guests.

"Well," Luke continued as they all sat at the long table. "You want to bet on it or what?"

"What's in it for you?" Noah asked, glancing out the window to see a squirrel run up a tree. Off in the distance he caught a glimpse of Amy, gesticulating with her hands like she always did as she showed another newbie around the resort. Noah caught the way Jared was watching her, his eyes glued on Amy's ass.

Noah looked back at Luke in time to see a sly grin slide across his face. "Your motorcycle."

"What the hell?" Noah's head jerked back. "You want my bike?"

"Yes. Not the one you're riding. I want that piece of

crap you keep in the garage.”

“What the fuck do you want with that?” Noah swallowed the bile rising up in his throat at the mention of his broken down bike, or rather Jonny’s bike. Jonny had loved that vintage motorcycle more than anything in the world. He’d purchased it years ago with the intention of rebuilding it. But he hadn’t lived long enough to get it up and running. Noah had spent the last few years tinkering with it, wanting to see Jonny’s dream through for him. Unfortunately, the parts for this particular bike weren’t only expensive, they were hard as hell to come by. He’d recently found the gearbox he needed, and had put a bid in on it, but pulled out at the last minute to lend the money to Jared when he’d found out Jared was in trouble. He’d lost the part to another bidder, and had no idea if he’d ever find another, but it was worth it. No way could he just sit back and let Jared get the shit kicked out of him, or worse.

“It’s taking up too much room in the garage, and I’m afraid my Porsche is going to get dented with all those parts you have lying around.”

Noah shook his head, hardly able to believe what Luke was suggesting. “What’s in it for me?”

“I’ll help you restore your bike. Either way I win because it gets the damn thing out of the garage quicker.”

“I don’t want you touching my bike.”

Luke met his glance, and they stared at one another over their food. After a long moment, Luke pushed back in his chair, and said, “Okay, fine.” He pulled his car keys from his pocket and dangled them.

Noah shook his head as he stared at the keys to the Porsche. “Are you serious?”

“Jesus, Luke, what the hell are you doing?” Jared asked around a mouthful of lasagna.

Without taking his eyes off Noah, Luke smirked and

said, "Don't worry. I know what I'm doing."

Shit, if Noah won Luke's car, he could sell it and get the parts he needed to finish the bike.

Noah angled his head. "Are you sure about this?"

Luke dangled the keys again. "This is how sure I am. So what do you say? Do we have a bet or are you too chicken shit?"

"You'll be gone all summer, how will you even know I got her?"

"I'll know."

"How?"

Luke arched a brow. "Because after one summer banging you, she'll come out the other end just as fucked up."

As he glared at Luke, he knew taking the bet was a shitty thing to do, but then again he was a prick, and pricks did shitty things.

He tossed a hunk of lasagna into his mouth and turned to Jared. "Tell me everything you know about her."

Chapter Three

Kathryn kicked off her heels and threw herself on her bed, her mind going over all the things she'd learned today. For the most part, her job consisted of preparing text for pamphlets, designing brochures, website updates, and helping her boss with corporate events. Next week, however, she'd be helping out with her first wedding, and she had to admit she was looking forward to being away from the desk.

A knock at her door had her jumping to her feet. She pulled it open to find Amy on the other side. Dressed in a pair of cute short shorts, and a top that didn't quite reach her belly button, which had a butterfly piercing dangling from it, Amy came bouncing into her room.

She frowned and planted her hands on her hips. "Wait, why aren't you dressed?"

"Dressed? " Kathryn asked. "For what?"

"We're heading to the Cave." She slanted her head. "Didn't we already talk about this?"

"I guess...I don't really..." Her words fell off as Amy rifled through Kathryn's closet. "What are you doing?"

Amy pushed her dark hair off her shoulders, disappointment on her face as she puckered her lips. "Did you bring all work clothes?"

"I just…"

"Never mind." Amy grabbed her hand and pulled her into the hall. "We're about the same size. I'll lend you something."

"Wait," Kathryn said, as Amy pulled her down the hall. "I wasn't really planning—"

Amy shot her a grin. "Your graffiti guy will probably be there. I'll introduce you."

"Oh." As Amy dragged her into her room, which looked like a tornado had blown through it, Kathryn couldn't help but feel intrigued. Back at school she often wandered the art district, longing to be a part of it. She'd made a few connections, and was even invited to a few after show parties, but had always ended up turning them down. "Well, I guess I could come for a minute," she answered, curious to meet the artist behind the graffiti.

Amy pulled open her dresser and began tossing clothes over her shoulder. "Nope. Nope. Nope," she said. "Wait, here. Try this."

Kathryn stared at the cute, summery orange, yet very short dress she was holding up. "I don't think…"

"Don't be silly. This will look gorgeous on you, especially with your hair." Amy tossed the dress over Kathryn's shoulder, and then reached for the elastic keeping her curls in a ponytail. "I can help you with your hair and makeup too," she said.

"I don't normally do much with it."

"Well, everyone who's anyone will be at the Cave tonight. And if you want to have a little fun this summer, and by fun I mean snag the hottest guy before one of the locals get their claws into him, then we need to get you all prettied up."

Her thoughts instantly went to Noah, and she was

about to say that the most fun she ever had was sneaking out to the art district, when Amy cut her off.

"Noah will be there," Amy said smiling.

"Is that who you're trying to snag?" Kathryn asked.

"Who isn't?" she said, laughing. "But, actually I'm kind of into his friend Jared." She held her arms up and flexed her non-existent biceps. "He got buff over the last year."

Trying to appear uninterested in Noah or his friend, Kathryn shrugged and asked, "What makes Noah so special?"

Amy's dark eyes went wide, and Kathryn couldn't help but smile at how animated she was as she threw her hands in the air. "You've seen him, right?"

"Yes."

"He's so hot, and I mean come on, who doesn't love a bad boy?"

Before she could think better of it she began, "But Shannon..." When she realized what she was saying, she let her words fall off, not wanting to gossip. Lord knew she'd been on the other end of the gossip mill a time or two. Of course that was to be expected when she studied all the time, and had no social life. Her classmates just didn't know the real her, and people were always threatened by the unknown. Then again, *she* didn't know the real her either, had never had the chance to explore what she really wanted, who she really was.

Amy grabbed her brush and ran it through Kathryn's hair. "Noah is here for a good time, like most of us. We're young. That's what we do, Kathryn. We have a good time."

Kathryn nodded and swallowed the lump in her throat, because she feared she wouldn't know a good time if it smacked her over the head. "Life isn't just about having fun." As soon as her father's words left her mouth she felt like smacking herself.

Amy pursed her lips and looked at her, obviously putting her psychology skills to work as she stared into Kathryn's eyes.

"You're right, but what good is living if we don't have *some* fun, and cut loose once in a   while? So come on, let's show off those smoky eyes of yours, take the straightener to your hair, put you in something sexy, and go enjoy being young." Amy stood back and let her gaze move over Kathryn's face. "Do you have any idea how gorgeous you are?" Kathryn felt heat move into her cheeks. No one ever told her she was gorgeous before. "Noah isn't going to know what hit him."

"I told you I'm not—"

"Yeah, I know what you told me."

A short while later, she sat beside Amy on the shuttle that took them to the Cave. Amy pulled out her phone and they shared contact information.

"In case we get separated," she said.

Hoping that didn't happen, Kathryn watched the beautiful scenery fly by, and when the shuttle finally stopped near a shale beach area, over half the people got off. The warm summer air washed over her, and gravel crunched beneath her feet as they walked a path to the water, to where the fire was already blazing high. Feeling a bit nervous, Kathryn let her gaze drift to the horizon, admiring the streaks of pink and purple bruising the skyline as the sun set over the mountains. She took in the sandy shore and the rocks hugging the sides of the beach.

As if picking up on her unease, Amy nudged her and said, "Relax, Kathryn, this will be fun."

Kathryn nodded and exhaled slowly. "Why do they call it the Cave?"

Amy pointed to the rocks. "There's an alcove in the rocks over there." She wagged her eyebrows. "Great for when you're looking for a quiet place."

Music blared from the open hatch of a car that was backed up on the beach. People were talking and laughing loudly as they sprawled out on the roof and engine bonnet. They reached the fire and a cooler was shoved into her hand as Amy introduced her around. She spoke briefly to Emery, the newly hired maid, as well as to Mike, the guy who worked the front desk with Amy. Kathryn recognized a few of the people from the resort, as well as from her living quarters.

She sipped her drink and tried to relax as she made conversation with her coworkers. A short while later, Amy waved a guy with dreadlocks over. He was a local bartender named Trent, and after discovering that he was the graffiti guy, Kathryn found herself relaxing, losing herself in conversation with him. She was on her second cooler and feeling the effects of the alcohol when a motorcycle sounded in the near distance. She turned to see Noah climbing off and tried to ignore the rush inside her stomach.

"Noah, my good man," Trent said.

"You know Noah?" she asked Trent.

"Who doesn't?"

A shiver skipped down her spine just from saying his name. She hugged herself and turned to see Amy, who was grinning at her.

"Do you want an introduction?" Amy asked.

"Not really."

"You should probably say hello, considering you're going to be seeing a lot of him this summer."

"Why would I be seeing a lot of him?"

A twinkle moved into Amy's dark eyes. "Because you'll be sleeping beside him for four whole months."

Kathryn took another mouthful of her peach cooler, finishing it off. "I don't plan on—"

Amy laughed. "Relax Kathryn. I mean he's in the

room next to yours at the lodge."

"Oh."

Screams erupted beside her and she turned in time to see a girl get carried into the water. A commotion broke out, and all around her guys scooped up girls and tossed them into the waves.

"What's going on?" she asked, a bit woozy from the alcohol as her mind tried to sort things through.

"Initiation," Amy said. She grabbed Kathryn's arm and tugged her closer. "Unless you want to get dunked you'd better—"

Amy didn't get to finish what she was saying, because some guy picked her up by the legs and tossed her over his shoulder. Her purse fell to the ground and all she could see was the sand rush by as he ran with her. A second later he tossed her into the lake.

She screamed, and took in a mouthful of water. Submerged, the cold waves seeped into her clothes and chilled her to the bone. Thrashing and freaking out in the dark, she kicked her legs, her body flailing like a hooked fish as she tried to right herself. She continued to struggle, to get herself together, when someone grabbed her by the waist, and pulled her to her feet.

"Are you okay?" a deep voice asked as he anchored her body to his.

She took one look into the most gorgeous pair of blue eyes she'd ever seen and knew in an instant that she was *not* okay. In fact, she might never be okay again. The feel of his body next to hers sucked the oxygen from her lungs. As she gasped and gulped to refill them, she slipped from his hold and dipped back under the water.

Before she even realized what was happening, he fished her out again and threw her over his shoulders. The movement forced the water from her lungs as he carried her to the shore. He laid her out on the ground and tilted her head back. A second later his mouth was on hers.

Bursts of warm air filled her lungs, but she couldn't think about that right now. No, right now all she could think about was how hot his lips felt, how his mouth tasted like beer and cinnamon and everything nice. Unable to stop herself, she moaned, her nipples tightening as she wrapped her hands around his head.

He stiffened and inched back. Their eyes met, and when confusion morphed into understanding, he said, "I thought you were drowning. I was performing—"

"CPR," she rushed out, mortified. *Please ground, open up and swallow me whole!* "I knew that."

Good Lord, how could she think he was kissing her? She resisted the urge to slap her forehead for being so stupid. Of course he was performing CPR. He was a trained white water rafting guide. He probably did this kind of thing all the time.

He continued to hover over her, his mouth still so close. She was more apt to drown in the embarrassment flooding her than the lake water. Working to appear unaffected, she went up on one elbow, and wrung the water from her hair. Then she turned her attention to the floral dress clinging to her body like a second skin. She peeled it away from her hips. When it made a sucking sound, she cringed and tried to wipe away the makeup running down her face. Good God, she could only image what she must look like. So much for Amy spending hours on her hair and makeup.

So much for snagging the hottest guy...

"Are you sure you're okay?"

"I'm sure," she sputtered.

He narrowed his eyes, like he didn't believe her. "I thought you took in some water."

Moonlight spilled over her rescuer as her glance moved over his face, dropping lower to take in the leather jacket stretched over broad shoulders. She'd seen him twice today, and knew he was hot, but having him this close did the most ridiculous things to her body. Her brain practically shut down, and her mouth opened and closed repeatedly, once again mimicking a damned hooked fish.

Get it together, Kathryn.

He leaned over her for a long moment, staring down at her. He had a strange look on his face, like he didn't know whether to stay there or run the other way. Finally he said, "Come on." He climbed to his feet and pulled her up with him, placing his hand on the small of her back to guide her away from the water. She tried to concentrate on her walking. But it was damn near impossible to put one foot in front of the other when all she could think about was how good his fingers felt splayed over her back. He led her to a piece of driftwood, where his helmet lay in the sand. He sat and pulled her down with him.

He put his elbows on his knees, folded one hand over the other, and turned toward her, watching her closely. "Why don't you just take a minute."

"I'm okay, really."

"You don't seem okay to me."

She shrugged, trying for casual. "That's just because you don't know me."

"So you're not hurt?"

She forced a smile. "Only my pride."

After a long moment he let it go and gave her a playful look. "I'm Noah," he said, his voice a little deeper than it had been moments ago.

"I...know. I heard all about you."

He arched a brow. "Oh yeah? What have you heard?"

Before she could help herself, she said, "That you should come with a warning label." God what did she say that for? Clearly his closeness was messing with her mind.

He laughed out loud, and Kathryn couldn't help but smile.

"Sassy," he said. "I like that." He brushed his thumb over the droplet dripping down her cheek. "I guess I need to do some catching up then."

She inhaled his scent, warm sand mixed with leather, and tried not to choke on her tongue when she asked, "Catching up?"

"You know who I am, but I don't know a thing about you."

"I'm Kathryn, with a K."

"So Kathryn with a K," he paused, and ran his finger over the top button on her dress. "Before we get to know each other, I think we should get you out of these clothes." She clutched her dress and he grinned, a teasing look on his face. "Or at least get you by the fire until you dry."

"Oh, right." What the heck was it about this guy that turned her inside out? Everything that came out of his mouth made her think of sex. And she never thought of sex. No, that wasn't true. She thought of sex, she just never *had* sex. Which was horrible and embarrassing for a girl going into her sophomore year.

He stayed over her for a second longer, his gorgeous blue eyes moving over her face before he climbed to his feet. He took her hand and pulled her up with him. Their groins collided and her entire body convulsed. He must have mistaken the shiver for something else because he pulled off his coat and wrapped it around her shoulders.

"But I'm all wet," she said.

"I don't mind that you're wet."

She caught the lopsided grin on his face, the suggestion in his eyes. Okay, so her thoughts weren't just going in an erotic direction because the guy was hot. She was thinking about sex because everything that came out of his mouth *was* sexual. She was sure of it.

Once again his hand went to the small of her back. She took note of the way the girls watched him as they trudged through the sand, and when they reached the fire, Amy came up to her.

"Sorry Kathryn. I was going to go in after you, but stopped when I saw you were in good hands."

As her glance went to Noah's hands, hands that made Kathryn quiver without even trying, she instantly knew there was nothing *good* about them. This guy had bad boy written all over him, and any girl would be wise to keep her distance.

She gave a wistful breath, because Kathryn Lane, good girl extraordinaire, always did what was wise. Right?

* * *

After getting up early and tinkering with Jonny's bike, Noah climbed onto his own crotch rocket and took a ride. There was nothing he liked more than cruising through the mountains when traffic was nonexistent. He could crank up his speed and go fast, and if he was really lucky, outrun the demons.

He took a winding turn and thought more about Kathryn and the way she had disappeared shortly after they'd walked to the fire to dry her clothes. One minute they were all standing around shooting the shit, but when he turned to talk to a townie, she'd disappeared. He heard her rustling around in her room later that night, and had thought about knocking on the thin wall that separated them. Instead he climbed into bed, exhaustion taking over him. He crashed for a little while, until the blood-soaked memories pulled him awake at the crack of dawn.

After a long ride along the windy paths, he made his way into the town square. Everything but Edible

Matters, his favorite coffee shop, was closed at this hour. He drove past Randall's Market and headed toward Edible's. He needed a strong cup of java, but the clouds moving in overhead warned him it was time to turn back. His wheels weren't great on slippery roads, and he was only in a t-shirt. Kathryn had left with his jacket last night, and since he'd watched her suck back a few coolers with Amy, he didn't want to wake her this morning to get it. He was just about to make a U turn right in the middle of the street, when a flash of red caught his eyes.

No way!

As if thinking of her had suddenly conjured her up, he inched his bike forward quietly. He came up behind Kathryn as she browsed the shops on Main Street. She stopped outside a place that had paintings displayed in the window. She stayed there for a long time, her fingers touching the glass as she admired a local artist's work, specifically the paintings showcasing the Rocky Mountains.

He watched her, and it occurred to him that she seemed different this morning, a little more relaxed as she window-shopped alone. He took another moment to really look at her. This morning her hair was tied back, but when she angled her head, he could see that her face was free of makeup. There was no denying that she was pretty, even more so without all that crap on her big, green eyes.

He pulled closer to the sidewalk and revved loud. When she spun around, alarm on her face, he opened the mask on his helmet and asked, "Need a lift?"

She eyed him and then looked up and down the near empty streets. "Are you following me?"

He braced both feet on the ground, and folded his arms. "Maybe you're following me."

"Why would I be following you?"

"I could ask the same question."

"That doesn't even make sense," she said.

She planted her hands on her hips and Noah looked at her clothes. Last night she'd been in a cute dress that had showed off her nice legs, and today she was back in her work wear, with expensive shoes geared for the office, not a long trek into town.

He nodded upward. "You better get on, unless you want to get all wet again."

A noise crawled out of her throat as she tightened her blazer around her body. "It was nice when I left."

He snapped his fingers. "Things can change just like that around here."

A droplet landed on her forehead and she wiped it away. "I thought that only happened on the East Coast."

He grabbed his spare helmet and handed it to her. "Is that where you're from?" he asked, although he already knew she was. He'd lived on the East Coast himself for a couple years and had picked up on her accent.

"Yes," she said absently as her glance went from the helmet to the bike and then to him. She frowned. "Is that thing safe?"

"It's only as safe as the driver."

She inched back. "In that case—"

Laughing, he jerked his thumb behind him. "Come on, Kat, get on. I'll pop your cherry."

"What?" she asked, her body tightening. "What do you mean?"

Her reaction surprised him. "You've never ridden before right?"

"Right."

"So that's what I meant."

Her shoulders relaxed. "Oh, okay."

Something in the way she had reacted to his teasing struck him as odd, and he couldn't help but ask, "What did you think I meant?"

"Nothing," she said breezily, waving a dismissive hand.

"So what do you say, Kat? Want a lift?"

She exhaled slowly, and he could almost hear the wheels spinning as she glanced up at the sky, a dark threatening cloud directly overhead. "Fine," she said, and she fiddled with the helmet shield. "And it's Kathryn."

"Kathryn with a K. I know."

She adjusted her ponytail and pulled her helmet on. It seemed a bit too wobbly. "How's the head?" he asked.

She adjusted the helmet. "It's big, but it will be okay."

"No, I mean how are you feeling? You don't strike me as a drinker, so I figured you'd be a bit hung over this morning."

"I'm okay. Someone left an orange juice and a bottle of Tylenol outside my door."

He revved his bike slightly. "Good, then the noise won't hurt you." He shifted forward as she climbed on behind him. He showed her where to put her feet, and his cock sprang to life as she wrapped those long, sleek legs of hers around him. He waited for her hands, and when they didn't come, he reached behind him, grabbed them both and pulled them around his chest. He drew her arms around him only because this was her first time and he didn't want her to fall off.

He did a turn in the street, and her hands tightened around him as he headed toward their lodge. Her small fingers dug into his chest, but oddly enough, her touch didn't seem to bother him too much. With the ground slick, he took his time, but the rain falling on his shield made it tricky to see. He lifted it, letting the rain pelt his face as he negotiated the slippery road. Instead of pulling his bike into the staff garage, he continued past the resort, taking a back route to the ski hill.

He could hear the cranking of her shield as she lifted it. "Where are we going?" she asked, her breath warm on the back of his neck.

He took one hand off the handle bar and pointed toward the ski hill. "Up there," he said over his shoulder. "Shield down," he ordered.

He listened to her shield snap shut as he cut through the trees, dodged a few low hanging braches and took a sharp corner. He leaned into the bend and she pressed hard against him.

"Noah," she said, her voice uncertain as her thighs tightened around him.

His cock twitched. Jesus...

"Don't worry, Kat. I won't let anything happen to you."

A few minutes later, he stopped his bike at the bottom of the empty ski hill, which had been shut down for the summer. He adjusted the kickstand and they both climbed off.

Kat removed her helmet and rain fell as she looked around. He watched her, and when she blinked in confusion, he noticed the tiny flecks of honey in her green eyes. She pushed her wet bangs from her face, and swiped her tongue over her bottom lip. "Why did you bring me here?"

"I figured if you liked looking at pictures of scenery, you'd like this a lot better."

Blinking fat droplets of water from her lashes, she glanced at the mountains in the distance. "It really is beautiful."

"You haven't seen anything yet."

Noah pulled his keys out of his front pocket, and walked to the shed that controlled the lift.

She hurried up behind him. "What are you doing?" she asked, and he didn't miss the worry in her voice.

"Turning on the lift."

"We shouldn't be doing this."

"Why not?"

"Noah, we can't."

He unlocked the door, pressed a few buttons, and then flicked the switch. "Sure we can." He gave her a lopsided grin. "See how easy we can?"

She shook her head. "If we get caught...I can't lose..."

"It's okay, really. The lift needs to be turned on every now and then for maintenance. No one will think it's anything but that."

"What if we get caught?"

"What if we don't?" He started walking toward the lift entrance. "Come on."

He glanced over his shoulder to see her root her feet. "I don't think this is a very good idea."

"You will. Just wait."

A noise sounded in the woods. "What was that?" she called out.

Noah turned back and peered into the trees. "Probably just a wild animal."

"Like a raccoon."

"Yeah, or a bear."

"Oh, God!"

Turning, he headed toward the moving the conveyor. "Are you coming, or what?" he asked.

"Well, I'm not staying here alone with a bear."

Panting as she caught up to him, the cool rain coming down harder, they both jumped onto a wet ski lift. When she nearly slipped off he grabbed her, pulled her close, and held her in position.

"Hold this." He took one of her small hands and put it on the side bar. She gripped it like it was her lifeline, and while the panic on her face was cute, in a bid to relax her he said, "Don't worry, Kat. If we get caught, I'll tell everyone I kidnapped you and forced you to ride."

The tow carried them higher, and she looked down to see her dangling feet. "I can't believe I'm doing this."

"I know, but you want to, don't you?"

She shook her head, her wet ponytail flaring around her face. "No I don't want to. I'm not into breaking the rules."

"We're not breaking them, we're just bending them," he said.

She opened her mouth like she was about to counter, but as the chair carried them toward the sky, she glanced at the scenery and said, "Oh, my God."

"I told you."

He followed her glance, and exhaled slowly as they climbed the mountain, steam rising up from the ground below as the cold rain fell harder.

She wiped her eyes. "I wish it wasn't raining."

He shrugged. "I don't know," he said quietly. "I kind of like the rain."

"I do, too, but I want to take a picture, and I don't want to damage my phone."

"We can come back when it's not raining."

A noise crawled out of her throat as she cringed. "I can't imagine you'll ever get me to do this again."

He gave her a lopsided grin. "I bet there are a lot of things I can get you to do." She arched a dubious brow, and he rocked the chair.

She squealed. "Noah, don't."

"Don't what?" He stood up on the seat, and spread his arms, something he'd done a hundred times before.

"Get down, you're scaring me." When he sat back down and aimed a grin her way, she shook her head and laughed. "You're crazy."

"You know, I think that's the first time I've seen you smile."

"I shouldn't be smiling." Her glance left his and

searched the ground. "What we're doing is wrong." She poked her finger into his chest. "You're a bad influence."

"You have no one to blame but yourself. You knew I came with a warning label."

She whacked him, and he let loose an exaggerated oomph as he grabbed her hand to hold it. "You hit pretty good for a girl."

The smile she gave him felt like a sucker punch. Jesus, she wasn't just pretty, she was gorgeous.

She looked to the left, then right, taking it all in. Something moved over her face, something wistful. "I would love to paint this."

"Is that what you're into? Painting?"

She crinkled her nose, and that's when he noticed her freckles. Damn they were cute. "I don't really get to do it much."

"Why not?"

"Because..." She frowned, and her head fell forward, like the world was weighing her down.

"Because what?" he probed, even though he was pretty sure he already knew. The lift bumped and she fell against him.

"I'm a business student and that doesn't leave much time for anything else. I guess I'm all work and no play."

He exhaled slowly and stared off into the distance. "Believe me, I know what you mean."

From his peripheral vision, he saw her glance shoot to him, and when he looked back at her, she gave him a strange look. Despite his high IQ, it didn't take a genius to interpret the meaning behind that look. She clearly thought he had no idea what he was talking about. And why would she? He knew what she saw when she looked at him. He knew what he presented to the world.

"How would you know?" she asked. Then, as if

embarrassed by her judgment, she began to backtrack. "I mean..."

Coming to her rescue and turning the focus back to her, he said, "You should loosen up more."

"Yeah, maybe." She looked at him and her eyes said it all—he needed to do just the opposite.

He turned from her, and they both stared at the scenery for a moment, then Noah broke the quiet. "What is it you can't lose?"

"What are you talking about?"

"Earlier, you said you can't lose, but you didn't finish."

She hesitated for a moment and then said quietly, "My scholarship."

He nodded. "Do you attend Sanford?"

"Yeah, how do you know?

"You said you were from the East Coast, and Sanford's the best business school east of Toronto, so I just assumed."

Oddly enough, her school was only minutes from the one he used to go to. Both smack dab in the middle of the city, the two prestigious schools, Sanford and Kingsdale—one known for business and the other known for its top notch computer science program— were friendly rivals. And sometimes not so friendly, considering they took their sports very seriously.

Clearly not wanting to talk about it anymore, she plastered on a smile and asked, "So what are you into?"

"If I say your body, would you hold it against me?"

She looked confused for a moment, then when she got the joke—her, holding her body against his—she laughed so hard, he couldn't help but join her.

"What?" he finally asked.

Swiping the tears mingling with the rain from her face, she asked, "Noah, you can't be serious? You can't think a line like that really works?"

"You wouldn't believe how many times it does." He gave a sheepish shrug and said, "I guess you're too smart to fall for it."

Rolling her eyes, she said, "You guess?"

Seeing the smile on her face, and knowing he was the one who put it there, made him want to do it again.

"I really do love it when you smile. You should do it more often." He thought about that for a minute, and an idea formed as his eyes locked with hers, taking in the skepticism lingering beneath. "I think that will be my goal for the summer."

"To make me smile?"

"Yeah." He swept his hand toward the panoramic scenery below them. "Look where you are, Kat. I think you should have a little fun."

"Why?"

He looked at the mountains, and the light fog crawling up the rocks. "Because losing yourself in your work can be a dangerous thing."

She went quiet for a long time and then finally asked, "Do you think there's a happy medium?"

"Probably not."

She slanted her head, her gaze moving over his rain-soaked face. "You're kind of a strange guy, Noah."

Wanting to lighten the mood, he winked. "That's one of the nicer things people have called me."

Before she could respond, a big eagle flew in front of them, its massive wings stirring the heavy air.

Kat gasped and jerked back against the seat. Instinctively Noah put his arm around her, and pulled her close. "Careful," he said, not wanting her to slip from the wet seat.

Eyes alive, she shook her head and watched the bird as it circled them before flying away. "That...that...was amazing. Damn, I really wish I had my camera ready."

The joy on her face made him want to see the bird

again, too. "Like I said, we'll have to come back."

He settled against the seat with her as the lift began its descent. They both sat in silence for a while longer, lost in their thoughts as they took in the view. He shot her a sidelong glance and noticed her fingers didn't grip the side bar quite as hard as they had at first, and she now leaned forward, her eyes darting everywhere, cataloguing each new sight. After they slipped off the chair, he shut it down, and they climbed back on to his motorcycle.

"Ready?" he asked as she wrapped her arms around his waist without prompting.

With her mouth close to his ear, she whispered, "Thanks."

The softness in her voice had him spinning around, and when he caught the vivid honestly on her face, his throat tightened. The warmth in her eyes filled him with doubt as his mind went back to the bet. Shit. Now if he didn't follow through with it, he'd lose Jonny's bike, and he couldn't let that happen.

"Shield down," he said and then revved the bike to drown out the guilt niggling at his gut. They made their way back to the resort. He drove into his small space in the garage, and parked.

Kat climbed off and looked at Luke's Porsche. "Nice car," she said. Her glance went to his small workbench in the corner, where bike parts lay scattered about. "Yours?" she asked.

"Yup." The site of Jonny's bike made him think about the bet again. Guilt taunted him once again, but then he quickly shrugged it off. He needed to focus on his goal.

When she picked up a fuel pump to examine it, he put his hand on her back to guide her outside. "You better get out of those clothes."

She gave him a curious look, but instead of probing

she nodded and set the part back down. A few minutes later he stood outside her bedroom door, and braced his hand on the overhead jamb.

She peeled off her wet blazer and he couldn't help but look at the two damp spots on her white blouse. "Thanks for the lift," she said.

"Anytime."

"Seriously, Noah. It was…" she paused like she was looking for the right word, and then added, "…fun."

"You say that like you've never had fun before."

"Thanks again," she said, ignoring his remark, one that he knew was bang on. She was about to close the door, when he put his other hand on it to stop her. He dipped his head, and pitched his voice low. "Not so fast. You have something I'm going to need."

Her eyes widened, and he was certain he saw her nipples tighten beneath her blouse as she stood there staring at him, her jaw slack. "What...what do you need?"

He looked past her shoulders, and gestured with a nod. "My coat."

CHAPTER FOUR

Kathryn tried to focus on her readings, but she couldn't stop thinking about yesterday. Couldn't stop thinking about Noah. Even though he'd broken the rules by taking her up the mountain on the lift, the fact that he wanted to show her the landscape was very sweet of him. Actually, it surprised her that he would do something like that for her, considering he barely knew her. It also surprised her that he actually noticed her admiring the scenery painting in town. How observant of him.

She mulled that over and suspected there was more to the guy than met the eye. Still, she'd be wise to focus on her internship and forget all about him.

Lying on her bed, with her laptop open and the thick book on marketing in front of her, she flipped through the pages, struggling to focus. Just as she was about to nod off, her computer beeped, indicating she had a Skype call coming in.

She glanced at her laptop and, when she saw that it was her father, she sat up on her mattress and smoothed her hair back.

She pressed answer, and when her father came into view, sitting at his office desk on a Sunday afternoon, Kathryn said, "Hey, Dad, nice to hear from you."

"Kathryn," he said, small lines crinkling around his tired eyes. In that moment Kathryn's heart went out to him, the sadness in his eyes making her want to please him all the more. Her mind went back to five years ago to when she'd lost her mother—and he a wife. He'd buried himself in his work after her death. His only goal now was to see his daughter succeed and join him in his firm. Her heart thudded as she considered that, and suddenly Amy's words came back to her.

What good is living if we don't have some fun, and cut loose once in a while?

Kathryn had loved her mom and missed her dearly, but she really wished her father would find someone else who made him happy, someone who gave him a reason to get out from behind his desk. It would also be nice to see him focus on something other than her. If he were happy again, it might take the pressure off her to please him.

"I just wanted to check in with you to see how thing were going."

"Things are good," she said. "I don't start work until Monday, but I went in Friday to get a feel for things."

That brought a smile to his face. "Good for you. That shows great initiative."

Sitting on the bed beside her, her phone pinged, taking her by surprise.

She glanced at it, and when she saw the message, a message from Noah, her heart jumped into her throat and she couldn't help but wonder where he got her number.

Want to go white-water rafting?

"Kathryn," her father said. "Is everything okay?"

"Everything is fine," she assured him, ignoring the text. But when her phone pinged again, she felt the need to explain. "It's just one of the staff asking if I wanted to go rafting."

Her father's brows knit together. "Rafting? You're not there to go rafting, Kathryn. You're there to work."

"Which is why I'm going to text back and say no." She grabbed her phone and punched in the response.

"You should be taking this weekend to familiarize yourself with your new job."

At the stern tone in her father's voice, she dropped her phone like a hot potato and returned her full attention to him. He had braced his forearm on the desk and leaned toward the monitor, his brows lowered into a familiar countenance of displeasure.

"I am," she assured him, snatching up the colossal book on marketing and holding it up to the screen for him to see.

"Good," he said, nodding and leaning back in his chair again. When her phone pinged again, she could hear the displeasure in his voice when he said, "You should take care of that and get back to work."

After ending the chat with her father, she grabbed her phone, but couldn't help but feel a little excited to see that all the messages were from Noah.

She thumbed in the text. *I'm busy.*

Doing what?

Reading.

Zzzzzzz.

It's not boring.

I told you, you needed to loosen up and have more fun.

I am having fun.

What are you reading?

Where did you get my number anyway?

Amy. Now tell me what are you reading?

Not knowing whether to be thrilled or upset that Amy had given her number out, she looked at her marketing manual. She hesitated for a moment, her glance going to the Nicholas Sparks novel on her nightstand. He already knew she was all work and no play, and not wanting him to know just how boring Kathryn Lane really was she said, *"Nothing you would know."*

Try me.

Fine. Nicholas Sparks's latest.

If I give you the Cliff Notes version, will you come rafting?

Are you trying to tell me you read Nicholas Sparks?

Yeah.

You're not a very good liar.

And here I thought I was.

Hate to break it to you...

Now you've hurt my feelings. You can make it up to me by coming rafting.

I told you, I'm busy.

But you HAVE to come.

Why?

I didn't make you smile yet today. ☺

She laughed at the smiley face, and then clamped her hand over her mouth, wondering if he could hear her through the paper-thin walls.

If I open the door, stick my head out and smile, will you leave me alone?

Give me ten minutes first.

She listened carefully and heard him rustling inside his room. What the heck did he need ten minutes for?

She powered down her laptop, and shut her marketing book, and then looked down at the clothes she was wearing. Even if she didn't want to go rafting, which, when she really thought about it, kind of sounded like fun, she didn't have anything appropriate to wear. Most of her clothes were professional. She watched the minutes tick by and when her phone pinged and the text said, *Ready to smile?* she walked to her door, wondering what he was up to now.

She opened her door to find him standing there breathing hard, like he'd been running. With a crooked grin on his face, he held up a Nicholas Sparks movie. It wasn't the same as the book she was reading, but it was still a great movie. "If I promise to watch this sappy shit with you, will you come?"

Unable to help herself, she smiled.

His lids fell slightly, his features softening as his glance went to her mouth. "There it is," he said, his voice so low she had to strain to hear him.

Something in the quiet way he spoke, in the way his glance lingered on her lips when she smiled, made her knees go week. Despite thinking he looked utterly adorable, she drew a breath to center herself and said, "As much as I would enjoy watching you sit through that movie, I have work to do."

"It's Sunday. Work is for tomorrow."

Just then Amy and Jared came down the hall. Amy handed a big picnic basket to Jared and planted her hands on her hips. She eyed Kathryn. "Why aren't you dressed?"

"I'm not...I don't..."

Amy looked up at the ceiling and sighed. "Come on." She grabbed Kathryn's hand and practically dragged her down the hall.

When they reached her room, they began the "let's dress Kathryn" process again. Amy rifled through her dresser and pulled out a pair of shorts and a cute tank top. She held them out to Kathryn who reluctantly accepted them.

"I wasn't planning on going."

Amy cast her a pleading look. "Will you at least do this for me?" She grabbed Kathryn's hands. "Come on, I'm really into Jared, and want to spend some time with him. But I'm not going to go if you don't."

Kathryn didn't really know girlfriend protocol, considering she had only acquaintances at school. There hadn't been time to form friendships. A part of her suddenly resented having been deprived of such a common part of her girlhood. "Why do you need me there?"

"Because," Amy said, drawing out that one word. "It makes it more fun and I don't want to be a third wheel. Besides, I think Noah is into you."

A secret thrill moved through her. "Well, I'm not—"

"I know, I know, but please do this for me. I would do it for you."

God, how could she say no when Amy was always so nice to her? It was the closest she'd ever come to having a best friend. "Fine, I'll go."

Amy squealed. "Thanks, Kat. I'll make it up to you. I promise."

She was about to tell her it was Kathryn, but stopped herself. The nickname was actually growing on her.

When she walked back to her room with Amy's clothes in hand, Noah leaned against the wall, and crossed his legs at his ankles. He cocked his head, laugher in his eyes when they met hers. "Told you so."

"And what exactly did you tell me?" She grabbed the movie from him.

His grin widened. "That I could get you to do a lot of things."

She shook the movie case. "Well let's see if you're still smiling when I make you watch this tonight."

"Is it going to hurt?" he teased.

"Yes, it is."

"If it hurts, you'll have to kiss it and make it better."

Rolling her eyes, Kathryn shut the door on him. She leaned against it for a moment and thought about what it would be like kissing Noah. Everything about Noah and his teasing did the strangest things to her insides. She sucked in a couple of quick breaths, then quickly changed her clothes and met the three of them in the hall. They took the stairs to the bottom floor. A mountain breeze rushed over her when she stepped outside. Noah came close and warmth invaded her stomach, but it had nothing to do with the hot summer afternoon and everything to do with the boy standing next to her.

"Are we taking the shuttle?" Kathryn asked.

Noah drove his hands into his pockets, pulling his swim trunks low on his hips. "I'd rather take my bike."

She looked at Amy, who nodded toward the garage. "You might as well go with Noah." She lifted the picnic basket like it explained everything. "I'm going with Jared in his car."

With that they all walked to the garage, and five minutes later, Kathryn had her arms wrapped tightly around Noah's chest as he negotiated his bike through the streets. She relaxed into him, and could feel a little bubble of excitement in her stomach as she breathed in his scent. God, he smelled so good, like leather, the beach and something uniquely Noah.

Honestly, as she thought more about these new friends she had made, friends who accepted her for who she was, she couldn't help but feel a part of something special, and maybe even a little flattered by Noah's attention. Girls flocked to him, yet he asked her, boring Kathryn Lane, to go rafting. And for some odd reason, she was the girl he wanted to see smile every day. None of it made sense to her, but she wasn't going to dwell on it like she normally would. Today she was just going to enjoy the outdoors, Noah, and being part of a crowd. Tomorrow she'd buckle down and get serious for the rest of the summer.

Noah pulled his bike into a parking space at Canyon Run, and they both climbed off. Jared squeezed his car in beside them. Kathryn took in the boathouse and all the boats chained up outside. Her stomach moved into her throat.

"It looks scary," she said to Noah as she wrapped her arms around herself.

"Ah, a rafting virgin," Jared said coming up beside them. "Don't worry, it's safe."

She pointed to the bruise still slightly visible under his eyes. "Isn't that how you got that?"

Jared scrubbed his chin and exchanged a look with Noah. "Yeah, something like that," he said, but Kathryn was smart enough to know it was a lie.

"Come on, it's going to be fun," Amy said, skipping past her. She walked up to the shop window that rented wetsuits and grabbed two, along with water shoes. "Let's get changed."

She followed Amy into the female changing area, and keeping only her bra and underwear on, she climbed into the tight wetsuit. Afterward, they locked their valuables in lockers provided. Then they met they guys, who were already suited up outside.

Kathryn stood at the water's edge and shaded her eyes. Equal amounts of excitement and nervousness moved through her. Good God, she could hardly believe she was about to go careening down a river with her life in Noah's hands. She thought about her first bike ride with him and his comment about breaking her cherry. It occurred to her that he was true to his word, that he could get her to do a lot of things she'd never done before. His hard muscles flexed as he went to work inflating the boat and putting it into the water. As she watched him, her body tingled, and she couldn't help but wonder what else he could get her to do...what else she would put in those capable hands of his hands.

Noah stood in the boat and tried not to rock it as he reached for her hand.

She held it back. "You're not going to do anything to scare me, are you?"

He held his hand over his chest and gave her, what she assumed, was his best innocent face. "I wouldn't dream of it. Scout's honor."

Kathryn pursed her lips. "Why do I have a hard time believing you were a scout?"

Amy climbed in and handed the picnic basket to Jared. He strapped it down.

Noah reached for her. "Come on, Kat."

Putting her hand in his, she let him help her into the boat. She pulled on a helmet and tied her life jacket as tightly as she could.

"All set?" Noah asked, grinning as she took a seat near him at the back of the boat while Amy and Jared moved to the front.

She grabbed her oar with one hand and held the rope going down the center of the boat with the other. A few minutes later they were going down a lazy river and she relaxed. She tilted her face to the sky, drinking in the sun. "This isn't so bad," she said, but a few minutes later, the river split. Noah went left, and the waves started picking up. "Oh God, maybe I spoke too soon."

"Start paddling," Noah said.

With Noah at the rear of the boat, guiding the way, she began paddling furiously, even though she had no clue if she was making things better or worse. The boat rocked, and her legs went up in the air. Her head practically landed on Noah's lap. When she squealed, Noah laughed, his blue eyes glistening as he helped her up.

She paddled like her life depended on it, but it was all downhill from there. The rapids grew strong and they bounced off rocks. Water splashed up and soaked her. Amy and Jared laughed from the front of the boat.

They bumped the shore, and the fast running water

carried them along the river. With her heart racing she looked over her shoulder to see Noah, who gave her an adorable smile. She turned back around and a half laugh, half cry crawled out of her throat when a cold wave splashed over her. A few minutes later the waves slowed, and they reached a quiet area of the river. Noah tapped her shoulder and pointed to the shore up ahead.

"That's where we're going," he said.

She nodded and tried to paddle toward it, but she was pretty sure Noah and Jared were doing all the work. When they were close, Jared jumped from the front of the boat and guided them in.

Still breathing hard, she set her paddle down and slumped in her seat, working to catch her breath. "That was...that was crazy," Kathryn said laughing.

She jumped from the boat and followed Amy, who held the wet picnic basket.

"Fun, right?" Amy asked as the two guys secured the boat.

"I'm still processing," Kathryn said.

"Let's go," Jared said, taking the basket from Amy. "I'm starving."

The two took off ahead, following a narrow footpath. Noah peeled open his wet suit and she tried not to stare at his chest as he walked toward her.

Kathryn jerked her thumb toward Amy and Jared. "Where are those two going?"

"Come on, I'll show you."

As they walked the narrow path, wildlife came to life around them and she moved in closer to Noah. His fingers brushed hers, and her pulse leapt. Working to sound casual, she asked, "You don't think there are any bears here do you?"

"Of course. You're in the middle of the woods. There are bears everywhere."

She made a tortured sound, and he laughed and

pointed down the path. "Don't worry, they're carrying the picnic basket." He grabbed her hand and tugged. "Which means if we don't hurry, either the bear will get the food, or they'll eat it all first."

They took off down the path and when they came to a clearing, Kathryn's breath caught. "I read about this spot in the brochure, but I had no idea we could get to it from the river." She spun around to take in. "This place is gorgeous."

Private picnic areas, tables and barbecue pits were set up in a lovely area with a view of the mountains off in the distance. They found Jared and Amy at a table under an umbrella. They'd spread out the food and drinks and waved her and Noah over when they entered the lush area. Mature trees and flowers fringed the picnic grounds, and off in the distance a hanging wooden bridge had been erected so guests could walk from one mountain peak to the other.

She breathed in the fresh floral scents around her. "Do people come here?"

Noah nodded. "The resort does lots of activities here, but today we have it to ourselves."

Kathryn slid onto the picnic table across from Amy, and Noah moved in close beside her, his warm wet body distracting her in sinful way. She dug into the sandwich, realizing how hungry she was after all that rafting, and swallowed the food down with a soda.

They made small talk as they ate, and when they finished, they put all their wrappers back into the basket. "Are we heading back now?" Kathryn asked.

Amy looked at her, then at Jared. She crinkled her nose and said, "I think we'll take a walk."

"Oh, okay." Kathryn made a move to get up, but Noah's strong hand came down on her lap. His big fingers splayed over her thigh, and her body instantly flared hot as he anchored her in place. She turned to him and when she caught the look in his eyes, understanding dawned. "Oh," she said again, feeling slightly embarrassed. "Right."

Amy squeezed her hand. "We'll be back in a bit. You'll be okay?"

"Sure," Kathryn said, breezily, trying to hide her discomfort.

Once they were out of earshot, Noah grabbed her hand and hauled her up. "Let's go."

She hesitated for a moment and inched back down. "Noah, I don't think…" God, did he expect her to go off into the woods and have sex too? She might seriously want to lose her cursed virginity, but this was all happening rather fast for her.

He stood over her and gave her one of his adorable crooked grins. "Don't worry, Kat. I'm not going to jump you."

She nodded, and for a minute couldn't tell whether the lump in her gut was from relief or disappointment.

"I just want to show you something."

"Like what?" she asked cautiously.

"You'll have to follow me and find out." She stood up, and Noah blocked her path. "Unless, of course, you want me to jump you."

"No!" she said.

Well, maybe…

He laughed and turned toward the woods. "Follow close."

She hurried after him, not wanting to get lost out here where wild animals roamed. Keeping close to his back, they traipsed through the woods, and she grew breathless the higher they climbed.

After a while they came to a small clearing, and steam rose up from a water hole in the rocks.

"It's a hot springs," he said. "Not too many people know about this place."

"Wow, it's amazing."

"Come on, let's get in." He shrugged out of his wet suit and then kicked it away, standing before her in nothing but a pair of boxer briefs that left little to the imagination. She felt a blush move into her cheeks and tried not to look, but how could she tear her gaze away? The guy was smoking hot, and everything about him reduced her to a giddy schoolgirl. Feeling a little breathless and a little dizzy, heat pooled low in her belly, and it took two locked knees to keep herself upright.

He slicked his wet hair from his forehead and his mouth curved. "Are you coming?"

Before she could answer, he jumped onto the rocks jutting out behind the hot springs. He climbed higher until he stood on a cliff, his arms wide. Sunlight streamed through the trees and fell over him, and her suddenly dry throat cracked. God he was so tanned, so cut. It was cliché, she knew, but he seriously took her breath away.

"What are you doing?" she asked, heat thrumming through her at the sight of him near naked.

"Diving in."

"That can't be safe."

"Do you always do everything that's safe?"

"Yes."

As she stood there staring at him, sure he was going to kill himself, he jumped. Good God, the guy was dangerous and reckless and being out here with him was probably a bad idea. But he made her blood burn hot and had her feeling things she'd never felt before. Things she *liked* feeling.

He finally came up from under the water, and she planted her hands on her hips and asked, "Do you have a death wish?"

He smirked. "You have three seconds to get in, or I'm coming to get you."

She looked at her wetsuit and thought about what she had on underneath. Her bra and underwear could easily pass as a bikini, but Kathryn didn't wear bikinis. In fact, she didn't wear anything sexy and rarely went swimming.

Rarely had fun…

Once again Amy's words came back to haunt her.

What good is living if we don't have some fun, and cut loose once in a while?

She bit her bottom lip, some suppressed, reckless part of her daring her to get in, to break free and have some much needed fun. Here in the middle of the woods, out from under her father's, her boss's, and the scholarship committee's eyes, maybe, just maybe, she could let her guard down.

"I don't have a bathing suit."

Steam rose around his body as he came closer. "You don't need one."

She grasped for an excuse, the reasonable, sensible side of her kicking in and warning her that getting in that water with a near naked Noah was a bad idea. "I don't want to get wet."

His glance moved over her wet hair and suit. "You're already wet."

She touched her hair and looked at her damp clothes. "Why is it that I always seem to be wet when I'm with you?" As soon as the words left her mouth, she realized how sexual they sounded. "I mean…" she began, completely mortified.

"One," Noah said.

"Wait, just wait," she said, kicking her water shoes off, and almost falling over as she rushed.

He swam toward her. "Two."

As equal mixtures of nervousness and excitement raced through her veins and a laugh bubbled up inside her. Hardly able to believe what she was doing, she unzipped her suit and shrugged it from her shoulders. Lord, she never did things like this.

But you want to, some inner voice said.

"Stop it, I'm coming," she said, feeling edgy, excited as she stripped down in front of this gorgeous guy.

Giving her no reprieve he continued to come closer. He stood up at the ends of the hot springs, and her breath caught when she watched the way the water glistened on his body. Her glance trailed one droplet, following it until it disappeared in the line of dark hair that led to his wet boxer briefs. Her eyes dropped to the hard ridges his underwear did little to hide and a tremble moved through her. Moisture grew between her thighs, and the harsh sound of her indrawn breath sent a bird into flight.

"Three," he said, his rough voice snapping her back to reality.

She squealed when he scooped her up and carried her out. She fought against him, expecting him to dunk her, but stopped when he gently lowered her into the water. Her hands lingered on his body, her fingertips reveling in the feel of his hard muscles as she found her footing.

"It's so warm." He let her go, and she pushed off him, swimming away. "Noah, it's so nice."

He swam toward her, going under the water and coming up directly in front of her. He pushed his hair from his face, fat droplets pooling on his long lashes as his blue eye met hers. He wet his mouth, and his voice was deep, low when he said, "Now isn't this better than sitting inside all day?"

As he crowded her, and his warm scent overwhelmed her, her brain practically shut down. Why again had she warned herself to stay away from him? He swiped his tongue over his bottom lip a second time and she spotted what appeared to be naked lust in his eyes as he dipped his head, bringing his mouth closer to hers. For a minute she thought he was going to kiss her; for a minute she wondered how she'd respond if he did.

Heat curled around her and her body trembled. "Noah?" she asked trying not to sound as breathless as she felt. Oh how she wanted to touch him. Wanted to trail her fingers over his muscles. Wanted to trace the outline of his tattoo. To ask who J was.

Apparently she wanted a lot of things.

He pushed her wet hair from her shoulders, exposing her neck. "Yeah."

He was so close she could feel the warmth of his body. He touched her arm, lightly trailing the rough pad of his thumb down the length of it.

Sexual energy leapt between them, but she wasn't sure what to say, how to act. She shifted on her feet, her stomach bumping against his groin. His nostrils flared and a low, animalistic sound crawled out of his throat.

"Noah," she said again, struggling to get her brain to work as she watched his Adam's apple bob.

"Hmmm…" he murmured, becoming strangely quiet.

She tensed. "Are you okay?"

"Don't think so."

"Why?" she croaked out.

She could see the hunger in his eyes, and hear it in his voice, when he answered, "Because I think I want to kiss you."

A nervous laugh caught in her throat, butterflies taking flight in her stomach. "You want to kiss me?"

"Yeah." He moved his mouth closer, so close she could taste the sweetness on his breath. She stood still, immobilized as he brushed his lips over hers, the warmth of his mouth doing mysterious things to her body. He inched back, his tortured gaze caressing her face as the muscles in his jaw rippled. "Kiss me back, Kat. Please," he whispered.

She stifled a moan as he put one arm around her back, hauled her hard against him and crashed his mouth to hers. As she kissed him back, his burning mouth pressed hungrily, his tongue fierce, demanding as it tangled with hers. Her body came to life as he splayed his fingers over her flesh. Her nipples tightened against his chest as he crushed her body to his.

Overwhelmed with the sensations racing through her, she wrapped her arms around him, but he grabbed them and anchored them to her sides.

She could feel his erection against her stomach, and she grew slick between her legs. Noah held her hands behind her back with one of his, while the other slid down her side, brushing along the outer edges of her breasts. She'd never been kissed like this before, touched like this, but she couldn't deny that it felt good, that she wanted more.

They stayed like that for a long time, exchanging long, heated kisses. She tried to loosen her hands, to touch him in return, but his grip was too tight, too strong. The sound in the nearby distance had them breaking apart. Noah inched back, and something conflicting moved over his eyes as they stared at each other for a minute. A moment later, his playful side returned.

"So, uh…have you changed your mind on me jumping you?"

She opened her mouth to answer, but had no idea what words were going to come out. Honestly, she couldn't believe that he kissed her, the way he seemed to want her. This guy could have his pick of girls, yet he was out here with her. It baffled her really.

"I…uh…"

Coming to her rescue he laughed and said, "Come on, I'm just kidding."

"Hey, how's the water?" Jared asked.

They both looked up to see Jared and Amy pushing through the trees, their hair a rumpled mess.

Amy stopped short at the edge of the water. Her glance went from Kathryn, to Noah, and back to Kathryn. "We're not interrupting anything are we?" She smiled, her look hopeful.

Jared didn't wait for the response. He tore off his wetsuit, jumped in and started roughhousing with Noah, each trying to take the other under the water.

Amy rolled her eyes. "Boys, they never grow up." She stripped to her underwear, jumped in and swam up to Kathryn, curiosity backlighting her eyes. "Well?" she whispered.

"Well what?"

"Spill!"

Kathryn swallowed, and stole a quick glance at Noah who was under the water. "He kissed me."

Amy squealed. "I knew it! I knew he was into you."

"Amy," she began, still unable to believe that kiss, or that a guy like Noah could be into a girl like her. "Do you think you could go shopping with me tomorrow night after work?"

Amy nodded excitedly, but before she could say more, Jared grabbed her by the waist and pulled her away.

After they all had a swim, the four made their way back to the raft. Dusk was approaching when they returned to the resort. Noah parked his bike, and together they walked back to their building. Kathryn yawned, and muscles she'd never used before groaned as she stretched her arms over her head.

"I'm beat." Walking slowly, a warm night breezed blew over her, and Noah moved in close, the heat of his body reaching out to her in sinful ways. She shivered and hugged herself.

"I guess this means I'll be getting out of watching a chick flick after all."

He looked proud of himself. Too proud. Kathryn

said, "I'm still going to hold you to it. Just not tonight. I need to get some reading done and rest up for tomorrow."

As she looked up at him, she realized that for the second time in her life she'd had...fun, and Noah once again got her to do something she had no intentions of doing. So much for not running in the same circles, because he seemed to be going out of his way to spend time with her.

They reached her room and he stood outside her door, his hands braced on the overhead jamb. "I guess I'll see you tomorrow, then."

She thought about her workday and her shopping plans with Amy later that night. "I'll be busy."

He grinned like he knew better. Like he was going to get what he wanted, one way or another.

"Do you always get everything you want?" she asked. Catching her by surprise, something dark and dangerous moved over his face and he went eerily quiet. Her gut tightened, and she reached for him. "Noah?"

He flinched but then the darkness disappeared as quickly as it had appeared; his playful side once again slipped back in place. "Yeah, I do," he said, and before he disappeared to his own room, he leaned in and stole a quick good-night kiss, one that left her standing at her door in a quivering mess and wondering what it was about him that had her doing things that were so uncharacteristic for her.

CHAPTER FIVE

Kathryn sat at her desk, going over the print copy on the brochures and checking for grammar. Every time she lifted her arms to her keyboard they ached, a constant reminder of yesterday's activities, of the kiss in the hot springs.

With a long list of duties in front of her, things that needed to be done before the wedding on the weekend, she worked to get Noah off her mind. She read over her list, then jumped from her seat to grab a file from the cabinet. A noise outside her office door drew her attention as she sat back down. She glanced into the hallway in time to see Noah walk by, or rather, slide by. Unable to help herself she laughed and then clamped her hand over her mouth, thankful that Shannon wasn't in the office to see her acting unprofessional.

He slid by again, and even though it was risky and inappropriate, she grabbed her phone from her briefcase and sent a text.

The moonwalk? Seriously, Noah?

He slid by a third time, looking oh so pleased with himself, but then Donald walked up behind him, and

Noah came to an abrupt stop. Looking like he'd just been caught with his hand in the cookie jar, Noah tugged on his work t-shirt and cast Kathryn a playful grin before giving his boss his full attention.

They spoke for a few minutes, but from her distance Kathryn couldn't hear the exchange. A few minutes later Noah disappeared, and she could only assume he was headed to Canyon Run for his shift. Donald looked into Shannon's office, his brow furrowed like he was trying to figure out what was going on, but Kathryn smiled politely and busied herself with her work.

The day seemed to drag on. Kathryn normally lost herself in her tasks, but tonight she was anxious to go to town with Amy. She was looking forward to picking up a few pairs of shorts and some t-shirts, clothing more suitable for after hour activities. For a brief moment she thought of her father and what he might say about these changes in her. Unease moved through her, and she suddenly found herself second-guessing her decision.

When the clock finally hit quitting time, she went to her room, still unsure, but when Amy flung her door open, standing there in a cute thank top and frayed shorts, she knew her friend wouldn't let her back out, even if she tried.

"All set?" Amy asked.

Kathryn drew a breath, let it out slowly, and before she could give it any more thought, before she let her doubts get to her, she blurted out, "Let's go."

They didn't bother to grab a bite at the buffet, since Amy wanted to take her to Grizzly's, the hottest club in town, at least on the weekends. The shuttle to town was fairly quiet, and soon enough they found themselves sitting at the bar inside Grizzly's. Kathryn was thrilled to see Trent was their bartender.

"What brings you ladies in here tonight?" he asked, pushing his dreadlocks off his shoulder.

"Two cold beers and two burgers," Amy said, rubbing her stomach.

Trent ran a cloth over the bar top. "You got it."

He disappeared to put in their order and Amy turned to Kathryn. "Now that we're alone, tell me. How was the kiss?" Kathryn felt heat move into her cheeks, and Amy rolled her eyes. "That good, huh?"

She nodded. "So what do you know about him?" Kathryn asked.

Amy shrugged and smiled at Trent when he delivered the beer. "Not much really. He came here three years ago the same time I did. He's a good guy, though."

"What makes you say that?"

"Jared didn't really get that black eye rafting."

"I kind of figured."

"He owned money to the wrong guys, and Noah bailed him out. Jared felt bad, because Noah had been saving forever."

"For what?"

"He didn't say, but I think it was for some part for his bike."

"The one that's in pieces in the garage?

"Yeah, I think. I think it belonged to a buddy of his. Someone he lost."

"J?" Kathryn asked.

Amy crinkled her nose. "J?"

"The tattoo on his arm."

Amy nodded. "Oh right. I don't know, he doesn't talk about it, but that would be my guess."

As she thought about that, Kathryn turned the conversation to Amy. "So you and Jared…?"

Amy smiled. "Yeah, thanks for coming yesterday, it was fun."

"Are you dating now?"

"More like we're fucking."

Kathryn choked on her beer and as she gasped for

breath, Amy patted her back and started talking nonstop about Jared, relaying almost every detail of their trip in the woods. Kathryn shifted uncomfortably, not used to hearing such intimate things—things that Amy clearly had no trouble sharing. A short while later, Trent brought their burgers.

"What are you doing later?" he asked Kathryn.

"I…just shopping."

"If you're still in town after dark, stop by Union Street." Kathryn recalled the graffiti on the brick walls lining Deerfield's art district. "I'll be hanging out with some of the guys." He made a fist and jerked his fist back and forth, mimicking the shaking of a spray can. "Getting in to some trouble. I'll introduce you around."

"Sound great." She looked at Amy. "Do you think we'll have time?"

"Sure."

Trent left and they dug into their food, the conversation bouncing back and forth between Jared and Noah. Oddly enough, every time she thought of Noah, she felt her stomach swirl. They eventually talked about their degrees and she came to learn that Amy wanted to specialize in helping teens. They finished their burgers and headed outside. Amy practically skipped along the sidewalk, pulling Kathryn into one of the many shops lining the streets. She grabbed piles and piles of cute clothes and shoes and gave Kathryn an honest critique when she came from the change room. Amy was so kind, always complimentary, so unlike the girls she knew. Even though she was strongly opinionated and gave advice, she never seemed to judge, leaving all final decisions in Kathryn's hands.

The more time she spent with her the more she liked her and knew that someday she'd made a great psychologist. During their shopping trip, Amy even picked herself up a few new items.

Deciding to leave on one of the cute pairs of shorts, they made their way down Main Street. Last stop on Amy's list was a lingerie shop, and Kathryn felt a little out of her element. She looked over the pretty clothing, running her fingers along the lace fabric.

"Oooh, Kat, look at this, you would look amazing in this." Amy pulled a pretty, see-through nightgown off the rack, and held it against Kathryn's body.

"I...don't know."

"Come on, don't tell me you've never worn lingerie for a guy before."

"Well…you see…"

"Oh, my God!" Amy said, her eyes widening as she flipped her hair from her shoulders. "I can't believe I didn't realize this until now."

"What?" she croaked out.

Other than the two staff, who were talking amongst themselves, she and Amy were alone in the store, but Amy lowered her voice anyway. "You're a virgin."

Embarrassment flooded Kathryn. "I…"

Amy touched her arm, her face serious. "Are you saving yourself for someone?"

"No, it's not that."

"Then what is it?"

Kathryn shrugged and absently ran the lace material between her fingers. "I guess it just never happened."

"So you want it to?"

"Well…yeah. I do. A lot."

Amy lifted her head high. "That settles it, then. You'll sleep with Noah," she announced matter-of-factly.

"What? I don't think…"

"He'll be perfect for your first guy. Believe me, you don't want to end up with some bumbling idiot who has no idea what he's doing." Amy cringed, like she had firsthand experience on the matter. She threw the lingerie over her shoulder and dragged Kathryn through the store. "Come on, let's pick out some nice things. You'll put one on tonight, invite him to your room, and once he gets a look at you bam, pop goes the cherry."

After trying on nearly ten pretty outfits, Kathryn picked her three favorites, the three that made her feel feminine and sexy. The thought of wearing them in front of Noah, however, made her nervous, excited...nervous.

Good God, did she really have it in her to slip into something so see through and blatantly invite him over to take her virginity?

Bags in hand they made one more stop at Randall's Market where Amy picked up some soda and candy. Night had fallen over Deerfield, and tomorrow was a workday, but Kathryn still wanted to go to the art district. They took a corner, and when she spotted Trent leaning against a street lamp, a few friends with him, they hurried along.

"Hey, Kathryn," he called out. "Come on over." When she reached him, he introduced her to his electric group of friends. One of the girls, Jasmine, with numerous piercings through her nose was on break from design school in Toronto, and one of the guys, Sam, was a machinist, who did machinist art and sold it locally. She talked with them for a moment and made plans to visit Sam's shop.

She turned back to Trent and he gestured toward the wall. "It's still a work in progress, but how do you like it?" he asked.

She looked over his Wildstyle graffiti. It was complicated and stylized and, to the untrained eye, probably extremely hard to read. She looked at the arrows, spikes and curves in the lettering, tracing her finger along them. "Trent, it's gorgeous."

"Gorgeous?" a familiar voice said from behind. "It looks like a big hot mess to me."

She turned to see Noah walking toward them, and the second their eyes met in the dark, heat arched between them. She gulped, sure that anyone within a fifty-mile radius could see the sparks, feel the heat they generated even from a distance.

"That's because you have no idea what you're looking at," she explained.

He gave her a cocky grin and nodded. "No, I know what I'm looking at. A blob."

Beside her Amy ripped into her bag of candy, and it gave Kathryn a fun idea. She looked at the cans of spray paint on the ground, and then shot Trent a glance. "Do you mind?"

"Be my guest."

"Perhaps I should draw something more on your level, Noah. Something you can identify with."

"Now this I can't wait to see." Noah leaned against the wall beside her and crossed his feet at the ankles.

Even though it was difficult to concentrate with him so close, she set her shopping bags down and went to work. She switched colors and cans when she needed them, and after a few minutes she could hear Trent and his friends laughing, clearly onto what she was doing.

When she was done, she turned to Noah and worked to keep the smile from her face. "This is what *we* call Appropriation, but *you* can call it an M&M."

Everyone laughed, including Kathryn, as Noah looked at the bag of candy Amy had just finished eating and then back at the wall.

"I think you just been schooled, Noah," Sam said. He patted Kathryn on the back. "Great work."

"An M&M?" He gave a slow shake of his head. "That says a lot about what you think of me," he said, working to smother the grin that reached all the way to his eyes. "Nice, Kat. Real nice." He laughed then, like he couldn't hold it back any longer, but when a siren sounded in the distance, all humor disappeared from his face and everyone took off running. A patrol light lit up the end of the street.

"Come on," Noah said, grabbing her arm.

Kathryn scooped up her bags and ran with him. They turned so many corners she had no idea where she was. He finally dragged her into an alleyway and pressed her against the wall. Breathing hard, he dipped his head and looked at her. "You okay?"

She nodded, even though her insides were in a big knot.

He scanned the alleyway, and then pushed against her. "That was fun, huh?"

Her heart pounded against her ribcage and her hair flared around her face as she shook her head. "I've never run from the cops before." She swallowed. Hard. "What if they caught me spray painting the wall?"

He shrugged. "They didn't."

A tremble moved through her. She let her head drop as she thought about getting in trouble with the law. It could have ruined everything for her. Why the hell had she picked up that can of spray paint in the first place?

Because it was fun, some inner voice answered.

"Hey," Noah said, putting his fingers under her chin to lift it. "You're pretty talented. You should paint more often."

"I'm never doing that again."

They heard a noise at the end of the alleyway, and when a light shone in, Noah dropped to the ground and pulled her on top of him. He put his mouth close to her ear and said, "Shh…"

She stayed completely still on top of him, her heart racing so hard she thought it was going to pop from her chest. A few minutes later the light disappeared and Noah let out a breath.

"That was a close one," he said.

"Too close," she whispered.

She shifted on top of him, and he groaned, his hands going to her back to hold her still. That's when she felt something grow against her pelvis. *Oh, God.*

Kathryn felt her own body grow needy as his cock thickened and pushed against her. "We…ah…we should probably move."

"Okay, he said, and rolled her on the ground until he was on top.

"I didn't mean like that," she whispered, but it was getting harder and harder to think as his weight pressed down on her. Not because she was becoming oxygen deprived, but because she was hyper aware of the way he was looking at her mouth, of how much she wanted him to kiss her again.

He slid his hand down her arm, brushing the outer edges of her breast. She quivered, his touch going right through her. Her breath grew shallow and she closed her eyes against the flood of heat pooling deep between her legs.

"Are you okay?" he asked quietly.

Her lids flicked open, and when their gazes locked, it fueled the flames inside her. "I'm feeling a bit dizzy."

"Maybe you're not getting enough air."

"Yeah, maybe," she said.

His grin turned wicked. "Maybe you need a little mouth to mouth again."

She didn't get the chance to answer him, because the next thing she knew his mouth crashed down on hers. His cock swelled against her body as he shoved his knee between her legs to widen them.

She moaned and it seemed to give him all the encouragement he was looking for. One hand went to her blouse, and he began popping the buttons. After he released the last one, he braced one palm on the ground beside her head and pushed himself up an inch. His nostrils flared as he looked at her cleavage, running his hand from her neck to her bellybutton. "Nice," he said, then moved his mouth to her breast, kissing her hard nipple through her satin bra. The heat of his mouth burned her body, and she put her hands on his shoulders, needing in the most unfathomable way to touch him.

He growled, and grabbed her hands, pressing them above her head like he didn't want her touch.

"Keep them there," he ordered. Desperate to feel his body, she was about to protest, but he dropped a kiss onto her mouth, stealing her ability to think with any clarity. He slid down her body, and tugged on her bra, freeing one breast. Even though the night air felt cool against her bare flesh, when he swiped his tongue over her nipple, her entire body went up in flames.

Oh, God it felt so good.

"You like that, baby?" he asked, but she was too far gone, too lost in the feel of his wet mouth wrapped around her hard bud to answer. As she arched into him, one hand slid up her thigh, and he rubbed her at the juncture between her legs. He growled and she could feel the tension rise in him. As sensations exploded inside her, it occurred to her that she never did things like this, but it thrilled her to see—feel—the effect she had on him.

His breathing changed, became labored as his mouth moved downward, his lips brushing over her hot flesh. His kisses felt like fire on her skin, and she began burning up, no longer caring that she was in an alleyway, spread out on the hard ground while he ripped at her clothes. He buried his face in her bellybutton and made a slow pass with his tongue. Moisture grew between her legs, dampening her panties.

"Noah," she cried out, her throat going dry. "Oh, God, Noah."

He popped the button on her jeans, and the hiss of her

zipper cut through the quiet of the alleyway. He pushed a hand inside her underwear and moaned, the heat of his mouth eliciting a shiver from deep within as he swiped his fingers over her clit.

"Oh. My. God," she cried out as a shudder overtook her body.

He stroked her again, his fingers circling her clit, and her pussy tightened, rippled. Feeling lightheaded, feverish, she rocked her hips, wanting more.

"That's it, baby," he murmured, his voice so deep she barely recognized it.

Pleasure forked through her and her brain began buzzing, the world closing in on her. He stroked her again, applying more pressure, and the buzzing grew louder, more demanding, and that's when she realized the sounds weren't coming from inside her head.

She froze, and Noah murmured, "Ignore it."

Some small coherent part of her brain reminded her that she'd just run from the cops, had left her friend to fend for herself while she made out with Noah in a dark alleyway. Amy didn't deserve this from her, and she could very well be in trouble.

"Noah," she croaked out. "I can't. Amy might need me."

Noah inched back and scrubbed his hand over his chin as he let loose a long, hard breath. He climbed off her and pressed his back to the brick wall. He just sat there for a minute, one leg bent at the knee, his arm resting on it like he was trying to get himself together.

"Okay," he finally said, and she reached for her purse. She pulled out her phone and sure enough there were at least six frantic texts from Amy.

Where are you?
Are you safe?
Why aren't you answering me?
Please be okay, Kat.

I'm at Grizzly's.

Come if you can.

With the mood broken between her and Noah, she texted back.

I'm okay. I'll be right there.

She looked at Noah. "Amy's at Grizzly's. I need to go."

He climbed to his feet and pulled her up with him. "Come on, I'll take you."

Feeling a bit awkward, a little unsure of herself after that fast make out session—Oh God, she still couldn't believe he put his hand down her pants, or how much she liked it—she zipped up her shorts and re-buttoned her blouse.

A few minutes later, both she and Noah made their way to Grizzly's. She noticed his bike on the street outside as they entered. Amy came running up to her. "Thank God you're okay."

"I'm okay," she answered, but Amy narrowed her eyes and looked her over.

"Are you sure?"

Striving for casual, she pushed her hair back in an effort to make herself look presentable, like she hadn't been rolling around with Noah on a dirty ground. "Yeah, I'm sure."

"You look like you could use a drink."

From behind her, Noah leaned in and put his mouth close to her ear. "I'll catch up with you later."

She turned around, but he was already headed out the door.

"Come on," Amy said, pulling her toward the bar. "Drinks are on me."

After having some fruity concoction with Amy and convincing her she was okay, they took the shuttle back to the resort. It was nearing her bedtime by the time she finished washing up and crawled into bed.

She pulled her sheets up and listened to Noah moving around inside his room next door. She wondered if he was going to text her to finish what they had started tonight. Her body quivered with the memories, and there was no doubt she wanted to pick up where they had left off.

She glanced at the bags on her dresser, her lingerie specifically. She considered putting something on and calling Noah over, like Amy had suggested. But just then a knock came on her door, and her heart jumped into her throat. She smoothed her damp hair down, and when she opened it to find a very sexy Noah standing there, her knees nearly gave.

"Hey," he said, those piercing blue eyes of his sucking the oxygen from her lungs.

"Hey," she responded around a tongue gone thick.

He made a move toward her, his fingers crawling around her waist to drag her close. "So I was thinking—"

Before he could finish her laptop dinged, indicating she had a Skype call coming in. She sucked in a breath, and glanced at her computer, her heart racing a million miles an hour. "That's my father. I have to take it or he'll worry."

Noah went quiet for a moment and then shoved his hands into his pockets. "Looks like technology is not my friend, tonight." He backed out of her room. "I'll catch up with you later, Kat."

CHAPTER SIX

Unfortunately for Noah, and his aching cock, later never came. Here it was Saturday morning, five days since he'd really spent any time with Kat, and he was sporting a bad case of blue balls. The only times he actually got to see her was when she was at her desk. This wedding she was working on was taking up all her free time, and when night rolled around he found himself crashing long before he heard her come in. He was beginning to wonder if she was avoiding him. Not that he could blame her. He'd gone at her like a damn tomcat in the alleyway the other night. But goddamn how he'd been dying to hear his Kat purr.

His Kat?

No, not really. She wasn't his. In fact, he was only interacting with her because of the stupid fucking bet Luke had backed him into, but he couldn't deny that he actually found himself looking forward to seeing her, and couldn't wait to hang out at the Cave tonight when she was finally done with all this damn wedding crap. A grin pulled at his mouth when he thought about how she schooled him with her artwork the other night. He was a

80

math and science guy, so yeah, when it came to art, an M&M really was the only thing he could relate to. Still it was pretty funny.

After a restless night, and being awake for most of it, he finally fell back asleep with the rising sun. It was nearing noon now as he rolled out of his bed and peeled back his curtain. He blinked against the blinding rays and knowing that Kat had been so stressed lately, he was thankful that her day to get out from behind the desk wouldn't be dampened by the weather. He cringed as he thought about Kat spending her life in an office. The more he got to know her the more he realized just how much she'd hate it. Underneath those business suits she wore, Kat was all spunk and humor, a girl full of talent. Damned if he didn't like that about her.

Then his thoughts turned to her father, and the way she'd stiffened up when he Skyped the other night. It was obvious he had a lot of control over her, had certain expectations from his daughter. She was clearly living up to those expectations, considering she was a scholarship student taking a business degree instead of following what she truly loved. Yeah, there was no doubt in his mind that Kat was living her father's dream and not hers. Not that this was any of Noah's business. It wasn't. Just like what he did with his life was none of her concern. Which meant he was going to keep his nose out of it. They were just going to have some fun this summer, nothing more.

Noah shut his curtains and powered up his computer. He spent the next few hours scrolling through the search ads looking for bike parts. He found a few things and flagged them to look at later. Right now his stomach was grumbling and he needed to get out from behind these four small walls.

Mid-afternoon was approaching as he made his way to the communal kitchen. He grabbed his cereal box and gave it a shake. Nothing. He opened the fridge, took out his orange juice container and took a huge drink from the spout, then jogged down the three flights of stairs to the bottom level and headed for the buffet. He walked past his garage and considered the bike parts he needed. He could pretty much find everything except the gearbox, but even if he did come across another one, his wallet was too tapped to get it.

He stepped onto one of the paths and walked toward the main resort. A flurry of activity taking place in the gardens behind the lodge caught his attention and he stopped for a minute, searching the crowd for Kathryn, but she was nowhere to be found. He caught a glimpse of Emery rushing around in a waitressing uniform and wondered if she'd taken on a new job. She stopped and spoke to Shannon, who was walking around with a clipboard.

Wondering where Kat was, he headed indoors. He strolled through the main lobby, and stopped to talk to Mike at the front counter to see if Kat was around. Mike had a worried look on his face as he pointed to Shannon's office.

Deciding to see if everything was okay, he crossed the lobby and stuck his head in, ready to throw on a goofy face to make her smile, but what he saw next had his grin melting, and his pulse leaping.

"Kat what the hell?" he asked as he entered.

She glanced up from her computer, a frantic look on her face. "The labels," she said, pushing her fingers through her hair. "I forgot to print the labels that go on the individual boxes of fruitcake." She shook her head. "Shannon is not very happy with me."

He relaxed a bit. "It's not the end of the world."

"Yes it is. I can't screw up, Noah! I just can't."

"Okay, so print them. The wedding hasn't even started. You still have time."

"No I don't. I'm out of time," she said, hysteria in her voice. "The cake is supposed to be on the tables already. And I can't print them." Shaky hands punched at the keyboard. "I can't even figure out how. Shannon has a new program for making them and I'm not used to working with it."

"Kat, it's going to be okay," he said, putting a little force behind his words in a bid to calm her down. She looked up at him and he noticed how white she was. Something inside him gave. He crooked his fingers and motioned for her to move. "Okay, get up."

"I can't get up," she practically shouted. "I have to figure this out."

Jesus Christ, is that how he used to look?

He stepped behind her and the wheels on her chair squealed as he pulled her away from the desk, giving her no more say in the matter. "I'll figure it out."

"How...you don't..."

"Just trust me on this, okay?"

She climbed to her feet, and hovered over him as he sat and started searching the programs. Since he knew his way around a computer with his eyes closed, it didn't take him long to find what he was looking for. "What are these labels supposed to say?" he asked.

She slid a piece of paper toward him. He read it, and then typed in, *Eat, Drink and be Married, Julie and Jack*, then added the date.

Feeling at home behind the computer, with that familiar rush he always got when surfing through files and solving problems, it suddenly occurred to him how much he missed this. Exhilarated, his heart raced a bit faster, and his fingers flew across the keyboard with a little more speed. "How many do you need printed?"

"Five hundred."

"You have the labels?"

She nodded and gestured toward the printer. "Yeah,

they're ready to go."

Noah hit send, and leaned back in his chair. "There you go. Crisis averted."

Kat rushed to the printer, and looked like she was about to cry when it started spitting out the labels.

"Noah," she began, her hands over her face. "Thank you," she mumbled.

He came up behind her and pulled her back to his chest, everything inside him softening. "Anytime."

She turned to him, curiosity and relief in her eyes. She looked at the computer, then at him. "How…how did you know what to do?"

He shrugged it off and instead of answering he asked, "Aren't you in a hurry?"

"Right," she said and started gathering the labels. "Thanks again, Noah. You saved me."

At the mention of him saving her, a lump formed in his throat. She must have sensed the shift in him because she cast a glance over his shoulder. "What?" she asked, her eyes narrowed as she accessed his face.

"Nothing. Come on, I'll help."

They both gathered up the labels and headed to the main kitchen area, where food was being prepared for the afternoon wedding. As the cooks and pastry chefs milled about, Kat led him to a long, stainless-steel table where little rectangles of cake sat in tiny boxes. When they passed by Tessa, the pastry chef, who was fussing over a three-tier cake, he stuck his finger out, pretending like he was going to taste the icing.

Tessa held a spatula up and waved it at him. "Noah, don't you dare."

Noah laughed. "But I'm hungry."

Tessa pointed to the fruitcake. "Have a piece of fruitcake, there's extra."

He tossed a piece into his mouth, and then after Kat showed him how to place the labels just right, he spent the next hour helping her. By the time they had labeled the last box, his stomach was on a full roll grumble, loud enough for everyone in the kitchen to hear it.

Big green eyes stared up at him, and when Kat gave him a genuine smile, one so sweet and grateful, something inside him tightened. "Thanks Noah. I don't know what I would have done if you hadn't come to my rescue." She looked back down at all the boxes and started packing them onto trays. "Now all I have to do is deliver these to the tables."

"Want some help?"

"No, I've got it." She stopped to poke him in the stomach. "And I think you need to go get something to eat."

"Right," he said. He dipped his head, and not caring who was watching, stepped into her personal space. "So I'll see you later, right?"

She nibbled her bottom lip, and her cheeks flushed, because clearly her thoughts were travelling down the same path as his. Tonight they were finally going to finish what they started in the alleyway.

"Yeah," she murmured, sounding breathless. "I'm just not sure what time I'll be finished up here."

"Come find me when you do."

Noah was about to steal a kiss when someone behind them cleared their throat. Kat went white again, her entire body stiffening.

"Noah," Shannon said. "Are you supposed to be in here?"

Noah spun around to find Shannon glaring at him. Her glance left his face, zeroed in on Kat, then returned to him.

"No ma'am," he said, then grabbed another piece of fruitcake and tossed it into his mouth as he pushed past Shannon.

"Kathryn," she said, and Noah could hear the

reproach in the older woman's tone as he made his way toward the swinging doors. "Those should have been on the tables already."

Leaving Kat to her work, Noah went and grabbed some grub. Since it was Mario's day off, he had to settle for a regular slice of pizza instead of two extra-cheesy ones. He scarfed it down and followed it with a soda.

Twenty minutes later, he was riding his bike along the mountains. He wasn't sure why but his thoughts travelled to his home in Ottawa, and to his mother, his father, and kid sister who all still lived there. As he thought about the life he had run away from after losing Jonny, a happy life he had no right to have, bile pushed into his throat.

Christ, he knew he never should have taken Luke's bet. Spending time with Kat, helping her on the computer, and seeing so much of himself in her had old memories clawing to the surface…had him *feeling* again.

Like her, he'd once been so driven, so focused, so determined to please everyone, to do everything to perfection, that he'd forgotten about what was important. He'd promised Jonny he'd pick him up from the party that night three years ago. But when his cell beeped, he'd ignored it, too lost in his computer coding assignment to pay any attention. Stone cold drunk, Jonny had left the party and walked home, although he never did make it. Just outside the apartment they shared, he stumbled into oncoming traffic. The car didn't kill him instantly though.

The crunching of metal followed by the ambulance pulled Noah out of his computer coding hypnosis—as Jonny used to call it—and he knew in an instant that something had happened to his closest friend. He ran outside and found Jonny pinned under a car. Jonny grabbed his arm and held it like it was a lifeline, like now that Noah was there everything would be okay.

Except nothing was ever okay again and when Jonny died that night, Noah died right along with him.

A half-cry, half-groan crawled out of Noah's throat and he squeezed the throttle, picking up speed as he raced through the winding mountain roads. Up ahead he came upon a car on a sharp corner. He passed the vehicle, despite not being able to see around the bend.

Jesus, why did he get to live and not Jonny? Survivor's guilt they called it. What-the-fuck-ever! It didn't change the fact that he should have pulled his sorry ass away from his assignment and picked up his best friend like he'd promised. He squeezed the grips harder, so hard his knuckles turned white and looked like they were going to punch through his skin. Fuck, if only he could go back in time and change things.

Thoughts of Jonny filled his mind, and he began weaving in and out of traffic like he was some goddamn suicidal maniac. A middle-aged douche in a minivan honked at him, but he ignored it, travelling at breakneck speed in an effort to outrun the demons. He drove long and hard, until his hands hurt from squeezing the handlebars so tightly.

Noah had no idea how long he spent riding the hills, but soon day bled into night and his insides were a total fucking mess by the time he returned to the resort. He sucked back a couple beers at the bar and gestured for another. He ignored the new bartender Alyssa when she shot him a concerned look. He held his hand up like he wasn't interested in conversation so she simply slid a third bottle across the bar top. He finished it off and, with the start of a good buzz going, he walked to his room, peeled off his damp clothes, and hopped into the shower. He grabbed a pair of boxers from his dresser, pulled them on and threw himself down on his bed. With his heart still racing from those blood-drenched memories, he draped his arm over his eyes and soon enough exhaustion, combined with three fast beers, pulled him under.

He tossed restlessly, kicking at the blankets, his body burning up like he'd been gripped by new deadly strain of the swine flu. He moaned, and flipped, the squeaking of his mattress briefly rousing him, until the demons pulled him back under again.

Somewhere in the back of his mind he registered knocking. The knock came again, louder this time, burrowing itself into his brain until he had no choice but to open his lids. What the fuck? He stared at his ceiling, willing the noise to go away, but whoever was out there refused to cut him some slack.

"Hang on," he grumbled.

He shook the buzz from his brain, threw his legs over the mattress and slicked his damp hair from his forehead. Dressed only in his boxers he shuffled across his floor, about to tell who ever it was to go the fuck away, but when he spotted Kat standing there, looking so pretty, and smelling so good, need tore through his gut like a runaway freight train.

"Kat," he said, pulling her to him.

The second her warm body pressed against his, he let loose a low growl. He roughly dragged his hands through her hair, tugging on it slightly to tilt her head back and open her mouth. God, that mouth. How he *needed...*

She was speaking, saying something to him but he couldn't comprehend, not when all he could think about was fucking her, losing himself in her, slaying the demons that continued to chase him. Swallowing her words, his mouth crashed down on hers, and he pushed his tongue inside. His brain swirled, raced, spinning the demons to the outer edges as sexual heat flooded him.

He deepened the kiss. Jesus she tasted sweet. So fucking sweet. He slashed his tongue against the sides of her mouth, and pulled her harder against him, his cock straining against his boxers. He moaned and tangled his tongue with hers, savoring the taste of cotton candy, sugar and honey all rolled into one. It was like a goddamn party in his mouth.

Her hands circled around him, her warm fingers running along his back, her long nails making him tremble, almost violently. He backed up until his knees hit the bed, and he grabbed her hands in one of his as he anchored them behind her back, running his other hand over her body, squeezing her tits, and driving a knee between her legs to feel the heat of her pussy.

She was breathing hard, taking gulping breaths, but he was too far gone to slow down.

"I need you naked," he murmured. Giving her no reprieve, he ripped at her t-shirt, pushing it upward.

His grip on her hands weakened and she wiggled one of hers free. Big, honey-flecked eyes met his as she helped him peel her shirt over her head. As it fell to the floor, some working part of his brain registered that she was in sexy black underwear—underwear that she'd worn for him.

Hands shaking, he ran his fingers along the tiny buttons lining the front until he reached her shorts. He ripped open the snap, desperate to get them off. He tugged at them, but they were too tight.

"Take them off," he growled, the muscles along his jaw aching as he clenched hard.

Her chest rose and fell erratically as she pushed them down her legs. A moment later she stood before him near naked, her long, sweet-smelling strawberry hair falling in waves over her shoulders.

He gripped a handful of her curls, and pressed a hard kiss to her mouth as his other hand went to the buttons lining the front of her lingerie. Jesus fucking Christ, why did they make them so small? He ripped them open and she gasped as they clattered to the floor.

Lust roared through him, her rigid pink nipples calling out to him in mind-fucking ways as they beckoned his kisses. He greedily pulled one into his mouth and sucked hard enough to leave a mark. He heard her whimper and once again she reached for him. He grabbed her hands, and held them to her sides as he sank to the mattress.

His mouth left her breasts and he buried his face in her stomach, pulling her floral scent into his lung. Jesus, she smelled good. He gripped her black matching panties and pulled them down her legs, then pushed his hand in between her thighs to spread her pussy lips wide open.

When he caught her pink sweetness, he leaned into her and licked.

"Oh, God," she cried out, faltering slightly.

Control obliterated, Noah grabbed her by the waist and pulled her on top of him. He flipped her over and pressed her into the mattress as his mouth found hers again. He kissed her hard, hungrily, as he drove a hand between her legs. He brushed her clit, then inserted a finger into her tight core. She clenched around him.

"You're so fucking tight," he murmured, and pushed his finger in and out, making her wetter, hotter. "I need to fuck you." Before she could even respond he pushed his shorts down and reached into his nightstand. He ripped into the foil packet, rolled on the condom and crawled up her body. He positioned his cock at her opening, and he buried his face in her neck, as he tasted her flesh, unable to get enough.

Oh, God he needed…

Her pussy lips tightened around his tip, but he needed to get deeper, needed to fuck harder. With single-minded determination, he pushed her hands above her head and shifted his body, grabbing her hips for better leverage.

He drew a sharp breath and then entered her. As he powered forward, his dick snagged on something and she cried out as he pushed through it, ramming his cock deep inside her. As her warmth wrapped around him, something niggled inside him, urging him to take a moment to figure out was going on, but with the demons closing in, he shut down his brain, and began to rock into her.

"So good…so fucking good," he murmured into her neck, his cock throbbing and pulsing inside her. He rubbed her tits, twirling her hard nipple between his thumb and finger, loving the way it grew taut. She was saying his name, at least he thought it was his name. He pressed his lips to hers again, his tongue plundering her mouth as he went up in a burst of flames.

Like a guy on a mission, he fucked harder, faster, yet still couldn't seem to get deep enough. Her aroused scent curled around him, and he breathed it in as his cock thickened. Fuck, he was so close. He plunged deeper, and slipped a hand between their bodies to rub her clit. Sticky, wet moisture coated his fingers as he rubbed. A moment later, her muscles clenched around his dick and when he felt her juices dripping over his cock, he gave into his own climax.

"Ah, Jesus," he groaned as a powerful orgasm tore through him. Trembling with need, he pushed deep and stilled. Every muscle in his body stiffened and he threw his head back, shooting a load into his rubber, as his cock pulsed inside her.

He collapsed on top of her, and swallowed against the dryness in his throat. His heart raced and his body hummed as it came down from the powerful climax. He buried his face in her hair and he drew a shaky breath. That's when he realized Kat was quiet…too quiet.

He lifted his head to see her, and when he caught the tears in her eyes, the pained expression on her face, everything inside him tightened. Christ, he'd hurt her. His heart beat faster, crashing against his chest as he lifted himself off her.

"Kat..." he whispered. She scrambled to grab the blanket at the foot of the bed. She pulled it up to hide herself, but not before he caught the blood coating her thighs. "Fuck," he said and swallowed hard. As the lust cleared, he looked at his blood soaked fingers, thought about the barrier he'd pushed through, and the stickiness between her legs when he rubbed her clit. A moment later his brain filled in the blanks. Holy shit. The wet heat on his cock wasn't because she'd had an orgasm, it was because he'd popped her cherry. "I...I didn't know."

"It's okay," she said, the flush on her cheeks spreading to her neck.

"It's not okay. I didn't know. I never would have..."
Oh fuck...

She rolled one shoulder like she was trying to shrug it off. "The first time is supposed to be the hardest anyway."

He tugged on his hair, practically pulling it from the roots. "Fuck, fuck, fuck."

"What?" she asked, her eyes wide, like she'd done something wrong.

"I shouldn't...we shouldn't."

"It's okay, Noah."

"No, Kat. It's not okay," he said, his voice getting louder. "You first time shouldn't have been like this, and it sure as hell shouldn't have been with me."

He could see panic in her eyes, when she said, "I don't understand."

"I need to get out of here."

"Noah, tell me," she said almost frantic, tears pooling in her eyes. "What's going on?"

He jumped from the bed and pulled up his shorts,

which were dangling around his thighs. Christ he hadn't even had the decency to removed them. What a fucking prick. He grabbed his jeans from the floor and climbed into them.

"Your first time…it shouldn't have been like that." He wagged his finger over the mattress. "Not like that, Kat."

"Oh," she said wide-eyed, her innocence ripping a hole in his gut. "What should it have been like, then?"

His heart squeezed. "Jesus Christ, you just don't get it, do you?" When she blinked up at him, he blurted out, "I went at you like a fucking animal."

She pulled the blanket to her chest tighter. "You did?"

"Yeah, I did."

"Why…why…" she began, choking on her words. "I thought…I don't understand…why would you do that?"

"Because I'm a fucking asshole, that's why."

Chapter Seven

A full week had gone by since Kat had spoken to Noah, and her insides felt like they were on an emotional roller coaster ride that had jumped the track with no controls to stop it. She wasn't exactly sure what was going on with Noah, or what had tripped his switch when he found out she was a virgin. She'd thought the sex was amazing, until he informed her that he went at her like an animal. Why would he do that? Why would he treat her that way, then call himself an asshole and run away? She didn't know. All she knew was that she'd felt completely and utterly miserable since she left his bed, and he'd disappeared from her life.

"Come on, Kat." Amy grabbed her hand and gave it a reassuring squeeze. "Everything will be okay."

Sitting on the shuttle next to Amy, Kat forced a smile. "I know," she said, even though it felt like her world was crashing down around her. She'd had a miserable week at work, and because she could barely concentrate, she'd screwed up a brochure she was working on. Once again, Shannon was displeased. Her father had called a few times, but she couldn't bring herself to answer. Once look at her, and he'd know she was not okay. The last thing she wanted to do was to lie to explain her misery.

"It's his loss, not yours."

"I just don't get it." Kathryn folded her hands on her lap. "I mean, the sex hurt, which I expected, but it was still good too, know what I mean?"

"Yeah, I do."

"I didn't think he did anything wrong, or that he was too rough, but I guess I have nothing to compare it to."

"That's it," Amy said, her eyes widening.

"What?"

"We'll find you someone to compare it to."

She shook her head. "No. I don't think I want to sleep with anyone else."

"Come on, Kat. We'll find someone at the Cave tonight." Amy tapped her chin. "I think I know just the guy."

"Amy, please. I'm done with guys."

The shuttle came to a stop, and they climbed off. The warm floral scent of the night air, combined with smoke from the fire fell over them as they walked to the shore. Amy opened her thermal bag and handed Kathryn a bottle before she added their drinks to the cooler. Kathryn twisted off the lid, and took a much needed drink, hoping the alcohol would help numb the emptiness inside her. Alyssa, the resort's assistant bartender came up to her, and they talked for a few minute. She'd come to learn that Alyssa was into photography and really missed developing her photos. As Kathryn thought more about that, and wondered if there was a way she could help her, the beach grew crowded, and she suddenly wished she'd stayed at home. Partying was the last thing she felt like doing. She only come because Amy insisted she needed to get out. Throughout the course of the night, she spoke to a few more of the resort staff, but pretty much kept to herself.

Just when she was about to find Amy and make an excuse to leave, Amy came pouncing over, a very cute guy on her arm.

"Kathryn, this is Caleb. He's a local, but we both go to university together. He's a football player," she added, like that changed everything.

Kathryn forced a smile and tilted her head. Lord, the guy was huge. "Hi."

He took a swig of his beer and said, "So Amy tells me you're into graffiti."

She cringed, thinking about her run from the cops. "I don't know if I'd say I was in to it."

"You were the one who painted the M&M though, right?"

"Yeah, that was me."

"It was very cool. I'm into painting, too."

"Oh really," she said, surprised to hear that from someone like him. Interest piqued, they started talking about their passions. A long while later the sound of a motorcycle caught her attention. Everything inside her stiffened as she turned her head to see Noah walking toward the fire. Their eyes locked for a brief second and her stomach knotted. She turned away from him, and tried to keep her knees from shaking as she continued to talk with Caleb, except Caleb had a strange look on his face as his glance kept straying to Noah.

"What's up with Noah?" Caleb asked.

Kathryn gripped the cooler so tightly she feared she was going to break it in her hand. Working to keep her voice even, she said, "I don't know."

"He's staring at you."

"Just ignore him, okay?"

"I don't think I can do that."

"Why?"

"Because he's on his way over here."

Kathryn's heart jumped into her throat.

"Caleb," Noah said as he stepped up to the two of them.

"Noah."

Noah's glance went from Caleb to Kathryn and back to Caleb again. Kathryn's entire body tensed when she caught the fire in Noah's eyes, the clench of his jaw. What had happened to the playful Noah she knew? The one who made light of everything and went out of his way to make her smile? The one who jumped in and helped her with the labels, zipping through files like it was second nature to him? She looked at him now and could sense something dark and dangerous brewing beneath the surface, something that once again reminded her that there was more to this guy than met the eye.

"Back the fuck off," Noah spit out.

Caleb held his hands up, palms out. "Listen, Noah, I don't know what's going on here, but I'm not looking for trouble."

Noah fisted his hands. "Yeah, well, too bad because you found it."

Caleb wagged his finger between Noah and Kathryn. "If something is going on between you too…"

"No, there isn't, but I just don't want you bothering her."

"Well hey, if nothing is going on then—"

"I said, back the fuck off."

"Noah, stop it," Kathryn said, unable to keep the hysteria from her voice. She searched the crowed for Amy, or Jared, hoping one of them could intervene and knock some sense back into Noah.

Before she could find them, a fight broke out in front of her. Noah went flying to the ground, but he jumped to his feet and retaliated. Soon the two were throwing punches, their bodies rolling around on the ground in a mass of blood and sand.

Kathryn screamed, and Jared came running over. "Shit," he said then gestured for a few guys to help. Once they peeled the two off each other, Noah spit blood and wiped his mouth.

"What is your fucking problem, man?" Caleb asked. "I told you I wasn't looking for trouble."

"Then stay away from her and there won't *be* any more trouble." With that Noah turned around and headed toward his bike.

Kathryn went after him. She grabbed the back of his jacket, and he spun around. His eyes, hard and dangerous, locked on hers.

She flinched and inched back. "Noah, what's going on?" He split blood again, and grabbed his helmet.

"Nothing."

"So, what, you don't want me but you don't want anyone else to have me?"

His blue eyes were colder than an East coast winter, and his voice was harder than she'd ever heard it when he said, "I never said I didn't want you."

With her gut completely tied up in knots, her mind raced, struggling to figure out what was going on with him…with them?

He climbed onto his bike, toed the kickstand into place, and wiped the blood from his face before pulling on his helmet.

She took a cautious step toward him. "I don't think you should be driving."

"I'm fine."

"You're not fine, you're acting like a…like a jerk."

He popped his shield and laughed. "Why don't you tell me what you really think?"

"What the hell is the matter with you?" she screamed.

Instead of answering, he started his bike, and took off, disappearing into the night.

With tears pooling in her eyes, Kathryn turned to find

Amy rushing up behind her. She put her arms around Kathryn's shoulders and led her toward the street. "Come on," Amy said. "Let's get you home."

"What is the matter with him?" she choked out.

"I don't know. He gets like this sometimes."

Close to an hour later, Kathryn crawled into her bed, her body exhausted. Except after seeing Noah, and that dark and dangerous side of him, her emotions were in a jumbled mess, her mind too revved up to sleep. She tossed restlessly, and heard Noah storm in sometime around two.

She listened to him bang around in his room, like he was drunk and knocking into things, or pissed off and throwing his furniture across his room. After a long time, he went silent and she wondered if he'd fallen asleep. With exhaustion pulling at her, she closed her eyes, and soon fell into a fitful slumber.

She hadn't been asleep long when a loud male voice pulled her awake. Her heart began pounding as she rubbed her eyes and looked around her room. What the hell was going on? Was someone in her room?

She listened carefully and then realized the noise was coming from the other side of her wall. Noah... He was yelling, crying out something she couldn't understand. Was he having a nightmare? Kathryn put her hand on the wall and drew a shaky breath. She listened a moment longer, and heard him mumble something about Jonny. Clearly the J on his arm stood for Jonny. What the hell had happened to Jonny, and did it have something to do with Noah's erratic behavior?

As she lay there with her ear pressed against the wall, Noah's cries stopped. A few minutes later she heard his door creak open. She sat up in her bed, her heart pounding, worry zinging through her blood. Moving slowly, quietly, she threw her legs over the bed, pulled on her robe, and slipped into her pink, fluffy slippers.

Padding quietly across her room, she inched her door open. She glanced up and down the dark hall, only to find it empty. Leaving her door open she tiptoed to the common kitchen wondering if she'd find Noah in there. She poked her head in and stole a quick glance around. Moonlight shone in from the window, giving her sufficient light to see Noah slumped in the chair beside the table, his hands over his face. Looking so incredibly troubled, so utterly lost he sat still…eerily still. Her heart squeezed in her chest at how miserable he looked. Whatever had happened to Jonny had taken a great deal out of him.

Kathryn backed up into the hall. She took a breath to get herself under control as emotions overwhelmed her and then made a noise, announcing her presence. She cleared her throat and stepped into the kitchen. He lifted his head, and stared blankly at her. Their eyes locked but she had the strangest sense that he couldn't even see her. She pushed down the unease welling up in her stomach and pointed to the fridge.

"Oh, I didn't know anyone was here," she fibbed. "I was just getting a drink."

He didn't speak. Instead he sat unnervingly still, his eyes following her as she walked to the fridge. She pulled open on the door handle, the refrigerator light spilling into the room. She grabbed a bottle of water, unscrewed the cap, took a long pull, and then put it back. She shut the door, plunging them into near darkness. With shivers skipping down her spine, she headed toward the hall.

"Kat."

The pain she heard in his voice stopped her in her tracks. She slowly turned around, and when their eyes locked again, and she saw raw emotions backlighting his baby blues, air left her lungs in a whoosh.

"Yeah?" she asked working to keep her voice steady.

"Want to go do something?"

She looked at the clock on the microwave. "It's three in the morning, Noah."

"Yeah, so?"

She tightened her robe around her waist. "I think we should get some sleep."

"Okay." He sounded so damn dejected, her heart missed a beat. She stood there a minute longer, and listened to his throat work as he swallowed.

She put her hand on the doorframe, worry moving through her. "Are you okay?"

"Can't sleep."

Something inside her softened and she found herself asking, "Where did you want to go?"

"I don't know." His brow lifted, hopeful. "Maybe a ride up the mountain."

She watched him for a long moment, everything inside her hurting for him. What was going on with him? "Give me a minute to get changed okay?"

She made a move to go, and paused when he said quietly, "Kat."

"Yeah.

"I'm sorry."

Her throat clenched. "It's okay."

"I didn't know. I wouldn't have…"

"Why wouldn't you have?"

"Because your first time shouldn't have been with me."

"I wanted it to be with you."

A tortured look moved over his face and he scrubbed his chin. "I didn't mean…"

"I know."

He stared at the ceiling, looking like he was a million miles away. A moment later he broke the quiet. "About you and Caleb…"

When he let his words trail off, she toyed with the

hem of her nightshirt and gave a confused shake of her head. "What happened? Why did you do that?"

"I'm an asshole." He forced a smile and her heart missed a beat. "Haven't we already established that?"

"Don't say that," she whispered. "You're not an asshole."

His eyes dropped and stared a spot on the floor near her feet. "You don't know anything about me."

She thought about his fight with Caleb, the biggest guy at the party. "I know you have a death wish," she teased hoping to lighten his mood a bit, but once again he fell serious.

His hand went to the tattoo on his arm, and he looked like he was a million miles away again when he rubbed it. "I have bad dreams. Sometimes I do things…" He let his words fall off.

"Are your dreams about J?"

His head came up. "What?"

She pointed to his tattoo and he stopped rubbing it.

"Oh. Yeah," he said, his voice so low she could barely hear it. "Jonny."

Her heart squeezed, making it hard to breathe as she waited for him to say more, but when he didn't she said, "Just for the record, there is no me and Caleb."

The tension in his posture relaxed, softening his features. "Okay," was all he said.

Kathryn hurried to her room to get dressed, and ten minutes later she was on the back of the bike with Noah, wind whipping her hair over her shoulders as they climbed the mountain. The streets were quiet, but he drove slowly through the winding turns. She tightened her grip on his chest, splaying her hand over his hard muscles. The air was cold and she pushed against him as a shiver moved through her. When one of his big hands closed over hers, rubbing to create friction, her heart swelled inside her chest and it occurred to her just how much she liked him. It also occurred to her that this was the only time he let her touch him. Why was that? Why didn't he like to be touched? She wanted to ask, but she was afraid it might bring up more painful memories.

After a long ride he pulled his bike off the road, and they both climbed off. He set his helmet on the seat and sat on the guardrail. He tapped the metal beside him. "Come here. You'll like this."

She sat beside him and hugged herself, wishing she'd worn more than a sweater. As though in tune with her needs, he pulled off his coat and draped it over her shoulders, then put his arm around her to pull her close. The warmth of his body reached out to her, and his scent, which was all over his coat, filled her with a different kind of warmth.

"Look," he said, pointing to the mountains in the distance. "Watch for a minute."

She sat there watching, then sucked in a breath when long fingers of golden light crawled over the mountaintop and lit up the valley floor below.

"It's beautiful," she whispered, guessing this was one of his go to places after one of his nightmares.

"Do you have your phone?"

"Right, pictures." She fished her phone from her sweater pocket and took a bunch of photos. "So gorgeous."

Noah reached into his coat pocket and pulled out his own phone. He snapped a few pictures and said, "You should paint this."

"I'd love to. I just don't have the supplies or the space."

They both fell silent, and after a long time she turned to look at him. "Noah?" she asked.

"Yeah?"

"What happened to Jonny?"

He jumped to his feet and walked to the ledge

overlooking the valley below. Body tense he scrubbed his hand through his hair. "I don't want to talk about it."

She stood and moved in next to him. She put her hand on his back, and when he flinched, like her touch physically hurt him, she pulled her hand away. "Maybe it will help."

"It won't bring him back."

"No, it won't. But maybe talking can help ease the pain."

He scoffed. "I deserve the pain."

"If you don't want to talk to me, maybe you can talk to a professional."

"No."

Pushing him a bit, she said, "Maybe you could talk to Amy. She's studying to be a psychologist."

"I don't need to talk to anyone. Jonny died, it was my fault, end of story."

"How did he die?"

He walked away from her and dropped onto the ground, his feet dangling over the ledge. "Kat, please, I don't want to do this…"

Kathryn sat down next to him. "Okay."

Noah picked up a small rock and tossed it over the mountain ledge. She listened for a long time before it hit. He threw himself down flat and stared up at the sky. She spread out beside him, watching the sunrise.

She breathed in the fresh mountain air. "I wish I could stay here forever."

"Why can't you?"

She turned to see him staring at her. "Because," she began giving him a playful smile. "Unlike you, I have responsibilities."

He looked at her long and hard. His mouth opened and closed, like he wanted to say something, like he was battling an internal war. Finally he asked, "If you hate business school so much, why do you do it?"

That statement took her by surprise. "Who says I hate it?"

"I do."

She frowned, not bothering to deny it. "My dad wants me to join his investment firm. I think he even has a nice accountant lined up for me to marry, too."

"And if you don't?"

"My mom died a few years back, and I'm all he's got. I feel bad, and don't want to disappoint him."

"I'm sorry about your mom."

Her heart squeezed. "I miss her so much." She shifted on the grassy embankment, and their hands touched. Hyperaware of their closeness, and the way their fingers were joining together, she looked back at the sky. While she wanted to know more about him, she didn't want to touch on another sore spot and upset him. Treading carefully, she began, "Are your parents…?"

"Both alive and in Ottawa."

"Is that where you're from?"

"Yup. I have a younger sister too." A small smile touched his mouth. "She's brilliant."

She looked back at him and as her glance moved over his face, she suspected his little sister wasn't the only brilliant one in the family. "Sounds like you're close."

He shook his head. "I haven't seen them since…well since Jonny died, and I moved here."

"Oh." He went quiet, and his fingers tightened around hers. "You must miss them."

He turned the conversation back to her. "So it's just you and your dad?"

"Yeah. We've only got each other." She plucked at the grass below her. "I just don't want to disappoint him, you know."

He rolled onto his side to face her. "What do you want, Kat?"

"I want to be happy, I want to enjoy life. I want to

have fun."

He smiled at her. "And when you grow up, what do you want to do?"

She shrugged. "If I could, I'd love to be a muralist."

"You could, you know. If you really wanted to, you could."

As she though more about that, she wondered if he wanted more out of life. "What about you, Noah? What do you want?"

He rolled onto his back. "I don't want anything."

"Do you want to stay here and work at the resort forever?"

"Maybe."

"Did you ever think about trying something else?" She remembered how skilled he was in front of Shannon's computer. How his eyes came alive as he helped her. "Maybe something with computers."

A noise crawled out of his throat. "Yeah, I thought about it."

With the sun climbing higher on the horizon, Kathryn yawned.

Noah jumped to his feet, and pulled her up with him. "You should get some sleep."

She took in his tired eyes. "You should, too."

They climbed back on the bike, and she held him tight, resting her cheek against his back as they drove. He pulled his bike into the garage, and she climbed off. Instead of following him to the door, she ran her hands over the bike he was restoring. She thought about what Amy had told her about Noah lending Jared the money, money he'd been saving for parts.

"How close are you to getting this up and running?"

"I'm in desperate need of a gearbox."

"Oh, yeah."

"This bike is a vintage 1940s Indian Chief, so parts are either hard to come by, or too damn expensive to buy."

Her glance went to the papers he had strewn across a small workbench. She picked up the piece of paper with an ad for a gearbox on it.

"I put a bid in on that one but had to pull out."

"So this is it, this is the part you need to finally get it going?"

"Yeah, this is it." He picked up the bike's old gearbox from the table and showed it to her. "The shop said this one was toast, and even if I could find the parts to rebuild it, it would cost a fortune. They told me I was better off finding a working one. There are still a few other parts I need, but I've not been in any hurry since I can't get a working gearbox."

"Interesting," she said.

"Come on," he said, grabbing her hand. "I know you don't really find this interesting."

"Sure I do."

He grinned. "You're not a very good liar."

"And here I thought I was."

She walked with him to the garage door and then stopped to take one last look at the bike. "Noah," she said quietly.

"What?"

"Was that Jonny's bike?"

He nodded.

"Is this how he died?"

"No." He went quiet for a long moment, then drew a deep breath and let it out slowly. "He was walking home from a party, and strayed right into an oncoming car."

"I'm sorry."

That haunted look returned to his eyes. "It's not your fault."

"Why do you blame yourself?"

"I was supposed to pick him up." She wanted to ask more, but he turned from her. He visibly shivered, like the memories had chilled him to the bone. "Let's get out of here."

Warm sunshine spilled over them as they stepped outside and walked back to their building. They climbed the stairs and Noah stopped outside his door. He opened it, and she was about to walk past but stopped when he said quietly, "Kat?"

"Yeah?"

He dipped his head, and touched the hem of her sweater, running the material between his fingers. His Adams's apple bobbed, and he gestured with a nod over his shoulders.

"Will you stay?"

She looked at the bed, then back at him, wondering exactly what he was asking.

As if sensing the question lingering on her lips, his hand moved to her face, his thumb lightly rubbing her cheek. "I don't mean like that. I'll take the floor if you want. I just…I'd just really like it if you'd stay."

Her heart squeezed as she looked into his troubled eyes, knowing it took a great deal of courage for this rough and tough guy to admit, in not so many words, that he didn't want to be alone.

"Okay," she whispered. "I'll stay."

He turned sideways to let her pass, and she walked into the room. She slipped out of his coat and draped it over his chair. Leaving her clothes on, she climbed into the bed. The fresh scent of laundry soap filled her nostrils as she snuggled in, her thoughts travelling back to the last time she'd been in this bed. Noah tore off his t-shirt, but kept his jeans on. He threw a pillow onto the floor and was about to flop down.

Kathryn shifted on the mattress, making room for him. "Come here, Noah."

He stilled. "Are you sure?"

"I'm sure."

He climbed in next to her and, knowing he didn't like to be touched, she resisted the urge to put her arm around him, to hold him tight and tell him everything would be okay—even though she had no idea if it would be.

"G'night," he said.

"Sweet dreams, Noah."

CHAPTER EIGHT

Noah awoke to a squirrel chattering loudly outside his window. As memories of last night came rushing back, he flipped over quickly, and relief rolled through him when he saw Kat lying there, her eyes still closed. He ran his hands through his hair, completely unnerved by how happy he was to find her there.

By rights she should have told him to fuck off last night. He didn't deserve her forgiveness or for her to spend the night after the way he had treated her. She was sweet and kind and far too good for an asshole like him.

As she breathed softly, he ran a long lock of her hair through his fingers, and that's when he realized how well he'd slept. Somehow having Kat there had kept the demons away, her warmth driving back the cold inside him. He thought about the things they'd talked about last night. He'd gotten personal with her and he swore he wasn't going to do that. But there was just something about her, something honest and genuine that made him want to know everything about her, and had him telling her things he didn't talk about with anyone.

Noah rolled onto his back and stared at the ceiling.

He thought about Luke and the stupid bet he'd made. A wave of guilt moved through him and a low groan crawled out of his throat. Shit, he was such a fuckup.

He felt a soft hand on his arm, and he turned to find Kathryn staring at him, those pretty green eyes of hers wide with worry. "You okay?"

"Yeah."

"Sleep well?"

He shook his head. "Not really, it was hard to get any sleep with all that snoring you were doing."

She laughed and whacked him with her pillow. "I do not snore."

He laughed with her, and grabbed the pillow from her. He reached for both her hands, and pinned them over her head as he climbed on top of her, like it was the most natural thing in the world for him to do.

Their laughter faded, and sexual energy arced between them as his weight pressed down on her, his cock growing thicker by the second. Like a skittish cat, she went still, perfectly still. Their eyes locked and when he read the question lingering in their stormy depths of hers, his blood cooled. No way, no how was he ever going to go at her like a rutting animal again. She deserved better than that. Just then his stomach growled, easing the tension between them.

"I need food." He rolled off her and stood.

She smiled. "You always need food."

"What can I say, I'm a growing boy."

Just then her eyes met with his swollen cock, and color moved into her cheeks.

Oh yeah, he was a growing boy all right—right between his legs.

He shifted and picked his t-shirt off the floor.

"I…uh…I guess I should get going." She smoothed her hair back.

He tugged on his shirt. "Do you have any plans for

the day?"

She walked to the window, pulled the curtains open, and folded her arms. "I should probably talk to my father at some point. I've been avoiding his calls and he's probably worried."

"Do you want to do that now?"

She turned to face him and drew her bottom lip between her teeth. "Maybe later."

"I have to go into Copperville, the next town over. There's a guy there who has some parts I need. I was wondering if you wanted to come."

"Sure. I guess. If you want me to."

"I do." He rubbed his stomach. "Now let's go get something to eat. I'm starving."

They made their way to the communal kitchen. Kat opened the door and frowned. "I haven't really stocked the fridge yet."

"Let's get something in town. I know this great café."

"Okay, give me a few minute to shower."

Noah sniffed, then made a sour face. Teasing her he said, "Please, take all the time you need."

She laughed and gave him a punch to the gut. "I do *not* stink."

God he loved it when she laughed.

He dragged his shirt away from his skin. "No, but I do."

Kat went to her room and Noah returned to his. He jumped in the shower, and as his thoughts returned to Kathryn, it surprised him how much he enjoyed her company, how happy he was that she had agreed to go into Copperville with him.

Thirty minutes later they sipped coffee at Edible's, his favorite cafe, and Kat dug into her cinnamon roll like it was the best thing she'd ever put in her mouth. He shifted, his cock springing to life as he considered that a moment longer.

She looked skyward. "This is so good. I don't usually eat things like this." She licked her fingers. "You really are a bad influence on me, Noah."

He grinned. "Good."

She laughed. "No, not good." She tossed another big bite into her mouth, then her eyes lit. "Oh, I've been meaning to ask you. Do you know if the resort has any spare space? I was talking to Alyssa and she's looking for a place to develop photography."

He thought about it for a minute, and remembered the winter maintenance storage building near the ski hill. "Yeah, I do. There is storage area near the skill hill. Winter stuff is kept there in the off season."

"Really, do you think she'd be able to use it?"

"Sure." He dangled his keychain. "I have a key."

"You have a key to everything. Management must really trust you."

"I guess."

"You must have had one hell of an impressive resume when you applied." She took a sip of coffee and wiped her mouth with her napkin. "What did you do before you came here?"

He looked at her long and hard and thought what the hell. She already knew a lot about him, what did it matter if she knew more. "I went to Kingsdale."

Her mouth fell open, and she stared at him, dumbfounded.

"Kingsdale, as in Kingsdale University on the East Coast, Sanford's rival school?"

"That's the one."

As she looked at him, equal amounts of surprise and respect dancing in her big eyes, he couldn't help but feel a bit pleased. "Close your mouth Kat. You might catch a fly."

"I can't believe it?"

"I take it that surprises you?

"It does but I guess it shouldn't." She shook her head, and took another bite of her cinnamon roll. "You have to be a genius to get in there."

He lifted his hands. "I wouldn't say genius. I mean, it's not like I can paint an M&M on a wall, or know what Appropriation is."

She laughed. "Noah, I'm impressed. Really." She went quiet for a moment, like she was remembering something. "That's how you knew your way around Shannon's computer."

"Yeah."

"When did you graduate?"

"I didn't." Deciding to change the subject before it turned back to Jonny, he stood, glanced at his watch, and said, "We'd better get going."

After a quick trip to Copperville, they returned to the resort. Kat went off to Skype with her dad, while he tinkered with his bike. Darkness fell over the mountain town by the time he went to grab a bite to eat and made his way back to his room.

He walked by Kat's room and heard her rustling about inside. He knocked, and his throat tightened when she answered. Dressed in her fuzzy, pink slippers, with a robe knotted around her waist, she smiled up at him.

Jesus she looked so sweet in those fuzzy slippers, so unlike the girls he normally went out with—well, at least the girls he went out with after the accident. He couldn't help but grin as he looked her over.

"What?" she asked, her eyes wide.

"Nothing. I was just thinking if you're not doing anything, that maybe we could watch that movie now."

She frowned. "I was going to do some work."

"Tsk, tsk. All work and no play…"

"And what about you, Noah?" she asked. "All play and no work."

He gave her a wink. "What a team we make."

She laughed and opened her door wider. "Okay, but just for a bit. I have to put together a big anniversary party for some very picky clients in a couple of weeks. They want some very specific artwork, and after the labeling fiasco, it's important that I don't miss a detail."

"What kind of art work?"

"They were married here thirty years ago, and spent their honeymoon hiking Stone Squaw Trail and camping in the mountains. They want the party room walls filled with local artwork to recreate the mood."

"They sound a bit weird."

"Eccentric is more like it. I have a limited budget and can't afford to buy any of the expensive paintings in town, so how they expect me to pull that off is beyond me. I certainly don't have the time to paint any myself or hire someone to pull of such a big job on such short notice. I've been scouring the Internet but so far can't find exactly what they're looking for."

Noah threw himself onto her bed, like it was exactly where he belonged. "I'm sure you'll figure it out."

She arched a brow. "Comfortable?"

"Yup." He patted the sheets for her to join him.

She sat beside him and powered up her computer. "Oh, I told Alyssa about the space you said she could have, and she's thrilled."

As he thought more about the winter maintenance storage building, and the big open room going unused, and idea formed. Perhaps Kat would get to paint this summer, after all. And maybe, just maybe, he could help her out with her work dilemma.

Her phone pinged, and she grabbed it and sent a text message back.

"Your dad?" he asked. Shit, he could only imagine what her father would say if he knew what Noah was planning. But truthfully she didn't belong in business school, or behind a desk. No, she had real talent and should be following her passion.

You should be following yours too.

"No, it's Alyssa. She said she'd call you tomorrow to discuss the space." Kat put her phone down. "I actually couldn't get hold of my dad. He was probably busy working."

"Like father, like daughter."

"Pretty much." She stuck the movie into her disc drive, adjusted her pillow and leaned back on the bed.

Noah got a sniff of her sweet scent and shifted closer. They remained pressed against each other as the movie played, but with Kat so close, her body so warm and soft, Noah was having a hard time staying awake. He let his eyes drift shut, just for a moment, but when he opened them again, it was morning, and Kat was snuggled in beside him.

Jesus, he could really get used to this…

Kathryn's eyes flung open to find Noah staring at her. Panic invaded her gut as she jerked her head to the left to check the time on her alarm clock. "Oh, God, no."

"What?" he asked looking past her shoulder.

"We fell asleep with the movie going, and I forgot to set my alarm. We're both late for work."

"Shit."

Kathryn jumped from the bed to get ready. "I need to move fast."

"Me too," he said, even though he was moving slowly. "I don't need to give Donald any more reasons to fire my sorry ass."

"Or Shannon mine." Kathryn grabbed her work clothes from her closet and ran to her shower. "I'll catch up with you later." She was just about to shut the bathroom door, when he stuck his foot in to stop her. She looked up at him, and before she even realized what was happening, he bent down and gave her a kiss on the forehead.

"Don't worry, Kat. It's not the end of the world."

"It will be if Shannon gets to the office first."

She closed the door and peeled her clothes off as Noah left her room. God, she really needed to get herself together. It wasn't like working in the resort's marketing department was her dream job, but that still didn't mean she didn't want to excel. The scholarship committee received an update at the end of the summer, and she had to perform to their satisfaction if she wanted her scholarship renewed. As she turned on the hot spray, another thought hit. What if she didn't perform well, what if she lost her scholarship? It would be the end of her world, right? Or would it?

What the hell was she thinking? She'd never had thoughts like that running through her mind before. Honestly, being with Noah was having a serious effect on her.

She grabbed the soap, and gave a quick wash. Twenty minutes later, damp hair pulled back into a tight ponytail, she practically ran to the main lodge. When she got inside, and spotted Donald and Shannon speaking outside her office, her heart fell into her stomach.

Shannon glanced at her watch as Kathryn approached.

"Good morning, Kathryn," she said.

"Good morning," Kathryn said cheerily and then smiled at Donald before he headed back to his office.

Shannon looked at her over her glasses. "Is everything okay?"

"Alarm troubles, but it won't happen again."

"The Carmichaels called about their anniversary party next month. They have some other very specific requests. You should probably get on that."

"Right away," Kathryn said, and stepped passed her.

The next three weeks passed in a whirlwind of activity for Kathryn. Her days were filled with work and getting the party organized, and her nights were filled with Noah. Besides a kiss on the forehead every now and then, he never once tried anything sexual with her. Instead they hung out after work. At times she helped him tinker with the bike, and he went with her into Deerfield while she gathered party supplies, and searched for reasonably priced artwork for the anniversary party. Every night, at the end of a long day, they fell into bed together, simply sleeping side by side. She was beginning to wonder if he just wanted to be friends, even though every time she was around him, her internal temperature rose and she ached to be in his arms again.

She thought back to the lingerie she had bought. Other than the sexy black outfit Noah had torn from her body a month ago, the other pieces were left untouched in her dresser.

A noise outside her office door had her glancing up, and her heart raced, hoping it was Noah.

Amy popped her head in. "So," she began. "I haven't seen much of you lately."

Kathryn waved her in. "I've been busy."

"Yeah, with Noah," Amy teased as she plunked herself down in the chair opposite Kathryn's desk.

Kathryn nodded. It was true that she had been busy with Noah, spending all her spare time with him, and thinking about him during work hours when she should be concentrating on the Carmichaels' party. Good God, she still didn't have the artwork they had asked for.

"So he still hasn't touched you since that first time?"

"No. I think he just wants to be friends."

"No guy just wants to be friends, Kat. They all want one thing. Maybe you should put on some of those slinky things we bought and make the first move."

"What if he doesn't want it?"

"Then you're kidding yourself. It's *all* Noah ever wants." Amy went quiet for a moment and then said, "Although he does seem a bit different lately."

"Different?"

Amy opened her eyes wide and waved her hands around her ears. "Yeah, like maybe he's not so crazy anymore. I think you've been a good influence on him."

"And here I thought he's been a bad one on me," Kat said.

"Nah, I think you two are good for each other." She glanced at her watch. "Quitting time." She climbed from the chair. "You going to the Cave tonight?"

"I think so, but I don't know for sure. Noah said he had a surprise for me and I have no idea what it is."

"Oooh, does this surprise involve naked bodies and a box of condoms?"

Kathryn laughed, and secretly hoped it did. "I somehow doubt it, but I'll let you know tomorrow."

Amy slipped into the hallway and gave a finger wave. "I only want to hear about it if moaning is involved."

Kathryn powered down her computer, anxious to find out what Noah had in store for her tonight. Honestly, she secretly hoped Amy was right, and that it involved naked bodies and a big box of condoms. It had been so hard being around him and not have him touch her, kiss her. For a brief moment she wondered if she should take Amy's advice and seduce him. Only problem was, after that first night he treated her differently, and she feared he'd reject her.

She hurried to her room, and after a quick shower stood in front of her closet, agonizing over what to wear. Since she had no idea what they were going to do tonight, she wasn't sure how to dress. She settled on a pair of shorts and a frilly, pink tank top. She applied a tiny bit of makeup to her eyes, then combed out her hair.

When a knock came on her door, her heart thudded, hardly able to believe how excited she was to see Noah. She pulled it open and he stood there looking so hot she had no idea how she would make it through the night if he didn't touch her.

"Hey," he said, dangling a bandana in his hands. "You ready?"

Her knees quivered as she pointed to the patch of material. "What's that for?"

"Your eyes."

"You plan to blindfold me."

He stepped closer, and cupped her chin. He lifted her face upward, until they were eye to eye, and when he wet his mouth, she wondered if he was going to kiss her. "You trust me don't you?"

She thought about it for a minute and then nodded her head. Noah might be a lot of things, but she truly believed he'd never do anything to hurt her. "I do."

"Good, now come on." He grabbed her hand and led her to the garage.

She took a look at his bike, which looked almost finished. "Are you almost there?"

"Still need that one part," he said, then twirled his finger, gesturing for her to turn around. She did as requested and he put the blindfold over her eyes.

"Not too tight is it?"

She fussed with it a bit. "No, it's okay."

He placed a helmet on her head, and she listened to him sit on his bike. Then he pulled her closer and helped her on. "Hold me tight, okay."

"Okay." With excitement bubbling up inside her, and having no idea what he was up to, she wrapped her arms around his waist, loving the feel of his hard muscles beneath her fingers.

When the bike finally stopped, he climbed off and

then helped her.

"Where are we?" she asked.

"You'll find out in a minute."

He began leading her somewhere, and she felt grass beneath her feet. She smelled pine and guessed they were in the woods somewhere. "Noah I don't know about this. You're not doing anything illegal are you?"

He laughed. "Trust me on this, okay?"

She grumbled and then clamped her mouth shut and listened as he fished his keys from his pocket. He unlocked a door and guided her inside. As he shut and locked it behind them she asked, "Can I take my blindfold off now?"

"Nope, just another minute."

He put his hand around her waist and led her through the building. They stopped and he held her shoulders, positioning her just right.

"Now you can take it off."

She peeled off the blindfold and looked straight ahead to see dozens of pictures framed and hanging on the wall. "What…how?" she asked. "Wait, is this the maintenance building where you set up Alyssa.'

"Yeah, and that's her work. She did it for the upcoming anniversary party you're working on. I know it's not the paintings you were looking for, but I still think these will work. She walked along Stone Squaw Trail, the same route they went on their honeymoon. These are the things they would have seen, so I'm sure they will love this."

She gave a slow shake of her head, her heart swelling inside her chest. "How…I don't understand."

"Let's just say we did each other a favor."

She threw her arms around him. "Noah, thank you. You have no idea how stressed I've been over this."

"Yeah, I do," he said laughing.

"You're a genius."

"Well, I don't know about genius, but I have heard the word brilliant tossed around after my name a time or two."

She laughed and looked at the pictures again, taking in the scenery, the wildlife, and the view from the mountain peak. "Amazing. And once again you've come to my rescue."

"One more thing." He turned her around.

"Noah," she whispered quietly, tears pricking hers eyes when she saw her second surprise. "Oh, my God. Noah, I can't believe this." She put her hands over her face, holding her cheeks as she saw the big wall all primed for painting. She looked at all the tubes of paint, the rolling pins, brushes, and art supplies. Then she noticed the picture pinned to the wall beside it. Noah had taken it with his camera phone the night they sat on the guardrail.

"You did this? For me?"

He shrugged like it was nothing.

Her chest rose and fell and her voice cracked slightly when she said, "No one has ever done anything like this for me before."

"You said you wanted to paint, so I thought you should paint."

CHAPTER NINE

Noah helped Kat roll on a thick basecoat to get the light blue backdrop she wanted. He looked at the paint splattered in her hair, on her clothes, and on her face. His heart twisted. Jesus, he loved seeing her so happy, so in her element.

"You're kind of a messy painter," he teased.

She laughed, and before he realized what she was doing, she rolled the blue paint over his arm.

"Hey," he yelled and jumped back. "You're going to pay for that!"

"Is that right?" She came at him again, holding the roller like it was sword and they were in a fencing match.

"Yeah, that's right," he said. He dropped his roller and, because he was bigger and stronger, easily took hers away.

She planted her hands on her hips. "Well that was kind of anti-climactic," she said.

His cock thickened as he pulled her close. "You want climactic?"

"I mean…I didn't mean…"

Jesus, she was just so sweet, so amazing. As she struggled for words, he pitched his voice low and asked, "Why don't you have a boyfriend, Kat?"

She went quiet for a long time, her eyes moving over his face before locking on his. "Who says I don't?"

He smiled, loving her smart mouth. A mouth that he would really, really love to kiss again. As she angled her head, her pupils dilating, it suddenly occurred to him what she meant. "Wait…are you saying…?"

She poked him in the chest and her voice was low, almost unsure. "Well, you are a boy, and you are my friend."

He swallowed the lump in his throat. Okay, there was no denying that he wanted her again. The last month had been pure fucking torture not being able to touch her, kiss her, bury himself inside her. But after the rough way he took her virginity, he knew he was a total fuck up who didn't deserve anything more from her.

She nibbled her bottom lip, like she was waiting for him to say something.

"Kat," he croaked out.

"Yeah?"

Going for broke he blurted out, "I want you. I want to be with you so fucking bad." He gripped a handful of his hair, and tugged on it. "Please, let me be with you again. I'll do it right this time…I promise." She opened her mouth but no words came. His insides twisted into knots. "Kat, please, tell me you want this, tell me you want me, and I'll make this right between us."

Both confusion and excitement moved over her face at the same time. "I didn't think you wanted me anymore," she said, her voice shaky.

"I've never stopped wanting you. Please tell me you want me too."

"I want you," she whispered.

Noah let loose a breath and brushed her hair from her

face, then gently rubbed his thumb over her plump lips. He leaned in and pressed his mouth to hers. Desire stirred inside him as she opened her mouth to him, granting him access. Their tongues tangled and he explored softly as he deepened the kiss, savoring the sweet flavor of her. He put one palm on her hip and gently ran it up her side, reacquainting himself with her body. His touch was slow, purposeful, because he was determined to take his time with her, to understand her needs and to make up for the last time.

After a moment, he pulled back and looked around the maintenance shed. "Not here and not like this."

"Noah?" she asked, her eyes confused.

"Let's go back to the lodge, somewhere comfortable."

She blinked. "Okay."

Noah helped her onto the bike, and her warmth wrapped around him as he dodged low hanging trees and sped back to the lodge. They rushed up the stair and a few minutes later they stood in her room. He touched her paint-soaked hair, and looked at his blue arm.

"Come with me."

He led her into her small bathroom and turned on the spray. He sat on the edge of the tub and crooked his finger. She stepped up to him, and her dark lashes flicked rapidly over those bewitching green, cat eyes of hers.

"Don't be afraid, Kat. Don't ever be afraid of me."

"I'm not. I just…I never showered with anyone before."

"I know." He peeled her shirt from her shoulders, and reached around to unhook her bra. A growl caught in his throat when her nipples tightened before his eyes. "But we've got paint all over us, and I don't want to make a mess of your bed." He grinned, and said, "Well I do want to make a mess of your bed. Just not like this."

She gave a nervous laugh. "I think you just like seeing me wet."

He groaned. "Jesus, I love it when you talk dirty."

Her cheeks turned pink. "Oh, I didn't mean…"

He looked at her near naked body and a tremble raced through him. "You are so beautiful."

"So are you," she said, her voice dropping to a whisper.

Holding her hands at her sides, he leaned in and gently swiped his tongue over one hard bud. She arched into him as his hands went to her shorts. The scent of her skin curled around him as he released the button, and then the zipper. Breathing in the tang of her arousal, he pushed her shorts and panties to her feet.

She kicked them off and he stood up, making quick work of his own clothes. Once they were both naked, he pulled her into the shower. With his cock throbbing, he looked at all bottles on the ledge, and squirted what he hoped was soap into his palm. He lathered his hands, and began washing the paint from her body.

He turned her so her back was pressed to his chest, and ran his hands all over her taking his time to cleanse every inch of her skin. His cock throbbed and pressed against the small of her back, letting her know how much he wanted her. She quivered under his touch, and once he had her all sudsy, he put her under the spray.

"Can I wash you?" she asked, her voice a bit hesitant.

"I'm okay." He lathered up again and quickly scrubbed the paint from his own skin.

Once they were clean, he climbed out and grabbed two towels off her shelf. He tied one around his waist and wrapped her in the other.

When he looked into her eyes and saw desire, his mouth found hers again and it was all he could do to slow himself down before he backed her up against that wall and pounded into her. She pressed against him, and his cock strained against the towel. A moment later the knot came undone and it slipped to the floor.

He was about to grab it when he felt Kat's hand on his cock.

"Oh, Jesus," he murmured.

She stroked him gently, like she was familiarizing herself with his length, texture. "So soft."

"Ah, not soft, Kat."

She chuckled. "No I mean the skin," she said once again reminding him of her innocence. "It's soft."

The warmth of her hands stroking him sent fire licking over his flesh. He clenched his jaw, the muscles rippling as moisture broke out on his body. As tension grew, he pushed her hair from her face and she looked up at him. Oh, fuck, how he needed her.

With pre-come pearling on his crown, he backed up, and her hand fell from his cock. She gave him a questioning look.

He briefly closed his eyes to get his shit together. "You have no idea what that's doing to me."

She rolled one shoulder and looked at his cock again. "I have some idea."

"Jesus…"

He grabbed his pants off the floor, yanked a couple condoms from his pocket, and pulled her into the room. Standing before her bed he kissed her, and when she unknotted her towel and let it fall to the floor, offering herself up so nicely, he took a shuddering breath. Determined to make this sweet for her, so fucking sweet that she'd forget about the last time, he cupped her ass, and lifted her, forcing her legs around his back.

Her mouth opened, and her eyes lit as he kneeled on the bed. He could feel the wetness of her pussy on his stomach as he shuffled to the middle. He fell on top of her, and her wet hair spilled across the pillow.

"Baby, I want you so much." He traced her face, her

jaw, and leaned back to run his hand between her breasts.

"I want you too," she whispered, her breathing uneven.

He looked at her and when he caught the longing in her eyes it touched something deep inside him. He gripped her hands and held them over her head as he buried his face in her neck. He filled his lungs with her scent, drowning in the taste of her. His heart pounded madly against his ribcage as his mouth traveled lower. He found one nipple with his tongue while his finger traced the other. He sucked and pulled and flicked until she was writhing like mad beneath him.

"So good," she murmured.

Heat curled through him when he left her breasts and kissed a path to her pussy, his palms sliding over her hot bare skin. His movements were slow, deliberate, testing her responses. The sound of her shuffling reached his ears. He glanced up to see her go up on her elbows, her face flushed, her eyes big.

Understanding she wanted to watch him, he pulled open her wet lips to find her dripping with desire. He ran the pad of his thumb over her clit, and her hips came off the bed. "Oh, God."

Christ, she was so responsive. His chest swelled, loving that he could make her feel good. "You like that?"

"Yes," she cried out and gripped the sheet. He eased a finger inside her, giving her time to get used to the fullness. He damn near shot off when her wet pussy swelled around him. He licked her clit, then circled it with his thumb. She began trembling, panting, growing slicker with each stroke.

She threw herself back down on the pillow and widened her legs even more. "Noah…I….oh, God, Noah."

He pumped a little harder, stretching her while he applied a bit more pressure to her clit. She thrust her pelvis forward and he knew she was close, so close. "That's it, Kat."

He swirled his finger through her slick heat, and applied more pressure to her clit. Her aroused scent swirled around him, and insane with the need to fuck her, he damn near lost it then and there. A cry lodged in her throat and lust exploded inside him as she came on his fingers, her wet heat dripping all over him.

"Noah," she whimpered.

"Yeah, I know, baby." He stayed between her legs, until she stopped trembling, and then he climbed up her body and flattened himself over her. His cock throbbed, and his muscles trembled, his control hanging on by a thread. Christ he needed her. Now.

"Kat, I really need to be inside you again."

She nodded and he grabbed the condom from her nightstand. He quickly rolled it on, and wound his fingers in hers, holding them over her head as he positioned his cock at her entrance. Her wet heat wrapped around his crown, and he took a deep breath, working to leash his control.

She closed her eyes, pinching them tight.

Blood pounded through his veins and his hunger for her made him quake. "Look at me."

Her lashes fluttered open.

"If I do anything that hurts, you tell me, and I'll stop, okay?"

She gave a tight nod. "Okay."

"I mean it, Kat."

"I will."

He pushed into her, offering her an inch at a time, letting her get used to his girth before he went deeper. She whimpered, and moved her hips, her body beckoning more.

With agonizing slowness he slipped inside, and once he was balls deep and could feel her heat scorch him, he let loose a growl. "Christ you are so hot and tight."

He began moving, slowly at first until she started to buck against him. He bit the inside of his cheek and powered into her. He gauged her reactions, and when a moan escaped her throat, her pleasure resonating through him, he pumped a little quicker, knowing he wasn't going to last long. His hips jerked as he moved in and out of her, escalating the tension inside him.

He drove a hand between their bodies, and rubbed her clit as flames surged through him. "I'm right there," he moaned, feeling the hot pressure of relief.

She gave a broken gasp, and the sound pushed him over the edge. His skin grew tight and his balls constricted, the pressure inside him coming to a peak. Her muscles tightened around his cock, and he drove deep and stilled. He threw his head back and released, drawing out the pleasure and savoring every last pulse as he came inside her.

Breath rushed from his lungs and contentment swamped him. Exhausted, he collapsed on top of her. "Jesus," he cried out, their shaking wet bodies melting together as one.

He rolled beside her and disposed of the condom. A warm, comfortable silence fell over them as they held each other close. He listened to her soft mewling sounds, and loved the way she purred for him, the way she felt in his arms. Stroking her hair, he drew deep breaths until his breathing returned to normal.

After a while, he shifted onto his side and looked at her, tenderness moving through him. "Hey," he whispered, his hand going to her stomach.

"Hey yourself."

He drew small circles with his fingers, and she trembled. "You okay?"

"I'm okay."

As he looked at her, his body grew needy. Christ it was insane how much he wanted her again. "Sore?" he questioned in a soft tone.

She crinkled her nose. "A little."

He lightly stroked her pussy, soothing it as he inched back slightly and worked to leash his cock. "Okay."

She grinned and drew his mouth to hers. "But that doesn't mean I don't want to feel you inside me again."

The rest of the week went by in a blur. Kathryn spent her workdays miserable at her desk, but her nights were filled with Noah. Noah kissing her, touching her, falling into bed with her where he would make gentle love to her all night long. The anniversary party went off without a hitch, except for when Alyssa, who was taking pictures for the Carmichaels, stormed out after talking to her father. The Carmichaels never seemed to notice and were thrilled with the photos.

Here it was Saturday night again, and she told Noah she'd meet him at the Cave because she had plans with Amy. Little did she tell him what those plans were. Sitting on the shuttle next to her friend, she patted her big beach bag.

Amy grinned. "Do you think he'll notice it missing?"

"I guess I'll just have to keep him distracted," Kathryn said.

Amy laughed. "My God, that boy *has* corrupted you." She wagged her brows. "But I like it. This is your summer break, and you should be having fun."

They hopped off the shuttle on Main Street and walked to the art district. When they came upon Sam's shop, which was nothing more than a little hole in the wall, they pulled open the door.

Sam glanced up from the metal artwork he'd been working on and smiled. "Hey Kat, Amy, nice to see you."

Kat looked at the piece, which was an artistic and delicate model of an old fashioned car. "This is beautiful, Sam."

"Thanks."

She looked at all his brass pieces and knew she'd be back to get something for herself. But right now she needed to talk to him about the real reason she was standing in his shop.

She pulled Noah's broken gearbox from her purse and held it out. "Any chance you can fix this?"

He looked it over. "Is this for Noah?"

"Yeah, I want to surprise him. Apparently the bike shop he went to told him this one was useless, and he's been unable to get a replacement. I thought that maybe since you're a machinist you might be able to rebuild it."

He grinned. "And what makes you think that?"

"I knew a machinist back home, and he used to manufacture custom parts for race cars. I know the shop told Noah this was no good without new gears, but what they failed to realize is that a good machinist could manufacture those gears."

He smiled at her. "Beautiful and smart," he said. "And it's not that they fail to realize it, it's just that they make money from ordering parts in and installing them."

She blushed at the beautiful and smart comment. "So do you think you can do it?"

He took it to his workbench, and opened it up. He looked at it for a few minutes and then nodded. "It's going to be a lot of work, but I think I can make new gears for it."

Kathryn heart jumped. "Really?"

"Yeah. Leave it with me for a bit, and I'll see what I can do."

"One more thing." She pulled a piece of paper from her pocket and handed it to him. Amy sucked in a breath when she saw the drawing Kathryn had done. "Do you know anyone who does engraving?"

Sam nodded. "You bet I do." Then he grinned at her. "Does Noah how lucky he is? Cause if he doesn't…"

She blushed again when she realized he was actually flirting with her. "How much for all this?" she asked.

"A lot. But I don't want your money."

She gave him a confused look, but before she could ask what he meant a customer walked in.

Sam greeted the man. "Hey there, Jack. I'm just finishing up with your piece." He shot Kat a look. "Are you going to the Cave?"

She nodded.

"I just need to finish up here, then I'll be heading over. I'll catch up with you then, and we'll go over payment."

As she speculated on what Sam could possibly want besides money, she and Amy went to Grizzly's for a bite. They ordered up their usual and talked quietly over burgers and beer.

Amy exhaled slowly. "I can't believe how fast the summer is flying by."

Kathryn swallowed a mouthful of tomato and nodded. "I know."

"In a couple of months we'll all go our separate ways again."

A knot settled in Kathryn's stomach as she thought about never seeing Noah again. She was getting kind of used to falling to sleep with him every night, not to mention waking up with him.

"You won't see Jared after the summer?" Kathryn asked.

"No, and this will probably be my last year here. I graduate next year so I'll be looking for something in my field."

As she mulled that over, and thought about her own

future, and Noah's, they finished their food and walked to the Cave.

She looked around for Noah, everything inside her aching to be held by him again, but he wasn't there yet. When she saw Sam, she made her way over to him.

"Hey, Kat," he said, talking over the loud music.

"I really appreciate you fixing the gearbox for me," she said.

"No problem. I don't mind doing favors for friends." He grinned. "I'm wondering if you can do me a favor in return."

She eyed him, having no idea what kind of favor he could want from her. "Okay," she said hesitantly.

"My niece is turning two next month and she loves Winnie the Pooh."

Kat nodded, confused and wondering where this was going.

"Everyone's talking about the mural you're doing and I was wondering, in exchange for me fixing the gearbox, if you could do a mural on her bedroom wall. She'd love it."

Kat's heart leapt. "Are you serious?"

"Totally."

She clapped her hands. "I would love that."

He pulled out his cell. "Great, what's your number? I'll text you with the details."

As they exchanged information, she heard Noah's bike. "I'd better go before he gets suspicious."

She walked over to him, as he made his way to the cooler for a beer. When she reached him, she noticed the possessive look on his face. "What were you talking to Sam about?"

She could barely keep the grin from her face, but she couldn't tell Noah about the job, not yet.

"Just art stuff."

"What kind of art stuff."

"You know what, I don't want to talk about Sam. I want to talk about us."

"Us?"

"I want to talk about the week you spent in my bed."

She pressed against him, and could feel his cock thicken. Heat moved into his eyes.

He slipped his hand around her head and drew her mouth close to his. "What about it?"

"Well, I love what we've been doing, but I also loved what we did the first time, too."

His brow furrowed and he inched back. "Kat, I was an animal."

She thought about the intensity inside him that night, how he had completely abandoned control.

"I realize I'm new to all this, and while I think soft and easy has its place, so does hard and fast."

He took a swig from his beer. "Jesus, Kat. You can't say things like that to me."

"Why not?"

"Because it makes me want to drag you over to those rocks and fuck the hell out of you, that's why. And I swore I'd never take you like that again."

She blinked up at him. "That's too bad."

His nostrils flared, and he grabbed her hand. "Are you serious? Is that what you want?"

She shrugged.

"Fuck," he said, setting his beer in the sand and capturing her hand. He practically dragged her across the beach, and excitement welled up inside her as he went all wild and alpha.

The air crackled with sexual electricity as he grabbed her by the waist, and turned her so she was facing the rock wall. He pinned her there and pressed up against her as he gripped her hands and positioned them on the rock above her head.

He caught hold of her hips and tipped her ass up as

he put his mouth close to her ear. "Is this what you want?"

"Oh, God," she cried out, her body trembling all over.

He ran his hands over her, squeezing her ass and pulling her shirt out from her shorts. He dipped his hand between her legs and as he widened her thighs, every nerve ending in her body came alive.

Her heart pounded erratically, as he reached around and unzipped her shorts. A moment later he pulled them to her feet, dragging her panties along with them. A cool ocean breeze washed over her, and it made it all that much more exciting to know she was doing something so naughty.

He gave a lusty groan and pushed his cock against her backside. "How about this, baby. Is this is what you want?"

She wigged her ass against him, loving the way he was coming unglued. He pulled her hair from her neck and ran his tongue over her flesh as he dipped between her legs, his fingers zeroing in on her clit. Her breath caught, and her legs weakened. God, he always knew just how to touch her. He pushed a finger into her, rubbing that magical spot inside that turned her into a quivering mess. A second finger joined the first, and she began panting.

Desire seared her insides, and when he pulled out, she let out loose a groan. "Noah...please," she said, not above begging.

He spun her around, and the next thing she knew his burning mouth pressed hungrily to hers. His tongue pushed inside and thrashed against her cheeks. Even though she ached to touch him, ached for him to *want* her touch, he held her hands over her head, grasping both her wrists in one of his big palms. He pushed against her, and shoved his other hand under her shirt.

He tugged her bra down, freeing her breasts, and bent his head to kiss her aching nipples through the material.

She sucked in a tight breath as his hand went back to her pussy. He pulled her lips open, then pushed a finger inside her. When she closed around him, his moan of pleasure carried on a night breeze. He fingered her for a long time, and she reveled in the sensations, traveling onward and outward through her body.

He dropped to his knees and buried his face between her legs. As his tongue seared her clit, she cupped his head and held him there, squirming against his mouth. He kissed her hungrily and heat spread through her body.

Moments before she was about to tumble into orgasm, he stood and kicked off his pants, his eyes burning with need. He reached for a condom, ready to tear into it when she stopped him.

"Not so fast."

His hands shook. "I thought you wanted it hard and fast."

"I do, but first this." She dropped to her knees, and pulled his cock into her mouth.

"Kat. Oh, Jesus, Kat," he said his voice thinning to a whisper.

She rocked against him, sliding him in and out of her mouth, tasting the come pearling on his crown. She moaned, having wanted to do this to him for so long now. He gripped a fistful of her hair and moved with her. She plunged forward, and then gagged.

"Easy, baby, not too deep," he whispered, pulling her hair back like he wanted to watch.

She licked the length of him, and cupped his balls, loving the feel of them in her hands.

"I love the taste of you," she murmured, as she looked up at him.

"Oh, baby, you're fucking killing me."

When she saw the raw lust, the agony on his face, she drew him back in. His veins pulsed as they filled with blood, forcing her to widen her mouth even more. She'd never done this before, but from the way he was trembling and gripping her hair harder, she guessed she was doing it right. She licked his crown, wanting to taste more of him, and when he let loose a tortured growl she sensed he was close.

"That's enough," he bit out, his voice rough and his breath ragged as he grabbed her shoulders to pull her up. He pushed her against the rock, and quickly sheathed himself.

With his nostrils flaring, and his eyes sparking blue fire, he gripped her hips and lifted her, slamming her into the wall as he powered into her.

"Yes," she cried out, loving the way he filled her.

Looking frantic, and on edge, he cursed under his breath and he pounded into her, long hard strokes that took her higher than she'd ever been before. As the depth of his penetration shut down her mind, she concentrated on the points of pleasure. God she was so lost in the sensations, so lost in him. His groin pounded against hers and she grinded her hips against his. Heat invaded her body, and her muscles grew tight, a tremor ripping through her like wildfire. A moment later she felt like she was shattering into a million pieces as her pussy clenched hard around his throbbing cock.

"Oh Noah," she whimpered, riding out the waves and never wanting the moment to end.

As her juices dripped over his cock, he slammed into her. His muscles bunched, and he gave a lusty groan. "You are so fucking hot," he murmured, then stilled inside her. She squeezed his cock with her pussy muscles, as he buried his face in her neck. His breath was hot on her skin as he moaned and released inside her. He stayed buried inside her for a long time, and when he finally pulled out of her, he remained pressed up against her body.

"Was that what you wanted?" he asked, his voice rough as his mouth settled possessively over hers.

She kissed him, her body clamoring for more, her heart clamoring for everything. "It's a start."

Breathing hard, he laughed and rested his forehead against hers. "I'm going to need a minute."

Chapter Ten

It was late afternoon on Saturday by the time Noah walked into his garage. For the past month he'd barely worked on his bike. He'd been too preoccupied with Kat. He grinned and his cock swelled as he thought about all the ways and all the places they'd been fucking.

He looked over his bench and ran his hand through his hair. "What the fuck?" He shifted parts around but his gearbox was nowhere to be found.

A noise at the door had him spinning around. Kat came toward him. "Hey," he said, dropping a kiss onto her mouth. "Have you seen my gearbox?"

"As a matter of fact I have. She held a box wrapped in Manila paper out to him.

"What's this?"

"Open it." She pushed the box into his hands.

"What's going on?"

"Just open it," she said, practically bouncing in front of him.

"It's not my birthday, you know." He ripped into the paper and lifted the lid.

When he saw his gearbox, confusion moved through

him. "What…what is this?"

"Your gearbox. I got it fixed."

"Fixed?"

"Yup, it's working now."

His heart squeezed so tight, it was difficult to breathe. "You did this? For me?"

"Yeah."

His glance moved over her face, and he drew a shaky breath. "But how…how did you know…how could you afford it?"

"I didn't buy one, I had your old one rebuilt."

"Rebuilt? How? I didn't even know that I could do that."

"I took it to Sam."

"Sam? Trent's friend?"

"Yeah, he's a machinist, and he didn't charge me a thing."

"He didn't?"

"Nope, just like you did a trade off with Alyssa, I did one with Sam."

His body tensed. "What kind of a trade off?" he bit out.

A huge smile lit up her face. "He heard about the mural I was doing and he asked if I would do one on his niece's wall for her birthday in exchange for this. I got my first job. I've been dying to tell you, but I couldn't until I surprised you with this!"

He scrubbed his chin, his entire body shaking, hardly able to believe she had done this for him. "Jesus, Kat."

Her smile fell. "What, you don't like it?"

"It's not that at all. I just can't believe you did this." No one had ever done anything like this for him before.

"Look," she said, turning it over in the box.

When he saw the engraving, the exact same one as the tattoo on his arm, a low pained noise crawled out of his throat. "Jesus…"

Her eyes widened with worry. "Noah?"

"Fuck, fuck fuck." He backed up until he hit the wall. He sagged against it, and let his legs slide out until he was sitting on the cement floor. He bent his knees, planted his elbows on them and gripped his hair as old memories ambushed him.

"Noah," Kat said, dropping down in front of him. "I'm sorry. I thought you would like it."

"It was my fault," he blurted out.

She shook her head, like she knew exactly what he was talking about. Her voice was low, careful when she asked, "How was it your fault?

"I was busy, working on a coding project. I was so into my work, I just forgot about everything and everyone. I forgot about what was important." He blinked his eyes and stared at the ceiling. "I don't ever want to be that guy again."

"So you became this guy instead. Once who tossed away responsibilities and became reckless as he walked around carrying guilt and blame."

"Yeah, I guess." He took a gulping breath, emotions pulling him under like a tidal wave, drowning him in sorrow. Tears stung his eyes and he swiped at his face. Shit, he was crying. He never cried.

Fuck, someone needed to kick him in the ovaries.

"Noah," Kat said again.

When a low growl crawled out of his throat she touched his arm. He flinched and she drew her hand back.

"Tell me about that night," she asked quietly

When he saw the genuine concern in her eyes something inside him ripped open, all the pain and hurt rushing though his blood. He gripped her arm. "He was on the ground, pinned under a car. When he saw me, he looked at me like he knew everything was going to be okay. That I would make it okay."

"Because you were always the responsible one?"

"Yeah." A strangled laugh caught in his throat as the memories shook him to the core. He pinched his eyes shut for a moment and gave a long pause before speaking again. "You and me, Kat, we're more alike than you know."

She nodded like she understood exactly what he was saying. "What else happened?" she asked, and he got the sense that she wasn't going to let up until he got it all out.

Noah tugged on her arm with both hands. "This is how he held me." He shook his head and swallowed hard. "I'll never forget it."

"And that's why you don't like being touched?"

"I guess. I don't know. It just…it just makes me remember, makes me *feel*." He looked at Jonny's bike then back at Kat. "When he died that night, something inside me died with him."

"Do you think this is what Jonny would want? Would he really want you walking around carrying all this guilt and grief? If he was here right now, what do you think he'd say to you?"

Noah swiped at his face. "He'd probably tell me to grow a set."

Kat smiled at him and his heart squeezed. "I miss him, Kat." He buried his face in his hands. "I miss him so fucking bad."

"I know you do."

"I wish I could go back and change things."

"I wish you could, too, but you can't, Noah, and nothing is going to bring him back, but that doesn't mean he's not here with you."

"What are you talking about?"

She put her hand over his heart, then touched his tattoo, and pointed to the engravings on the gearbox. "He's with you in spirit all the time. I don't know him, but I bet he'd want you to pick yourself up off this floor, get that bike working, and run every last demon over with it."

He couldn't help but laugh, a big hiccupping laugh. "You're probably right."

"I am right." He reached for her hand, and their fingers tangled. "Tell me more about him."

He squeezed her hand, and once he started talking about his friend, he couldn't seem to stop. As he shared his memories, good and bad, he could feel the tension drain from his shoulders, feel the pain leave his soul.

When he finished speaking, she shifted closer, and her heat, combined with the warmth in her eyes, had him needing so much from her. He cupped her head and pulled it to him.

"I need to be inside you."

"Come on. Let's go to my room." She climbed to her feet, but he dragged her to him.

"No. Right now, Kat. Right here. I can't wait that long."

He grabbed her hand and guided her to Luke's car. He reached under the car and grabbed a case with the key in it. He unlocked the door, and pulled her into the back seat. His mouth found hers and he kissed her. As he ran his hands over her body, she put hers above her head, and his heart twisted with need as he watched her. He inched back and looked into her eyes. They exchanged a long look, and then he took her hand in his and placed it on his face.

"Touch me back Kat. Please…touch me back."

"Noah," she whispered, her palm closing over his face. He leaned into her palm, absorbing her heat. His mouth found hers again as she touched him. Oh, Jesus, it felt so fucking good to be touched by her. As he reveled in it, lost himself in it, he pulled his shirt off to let her explore him. The softness in her fingers moved over his skin like a healing balm to his soul, lighting the darkness inside him and helping him to come to peace.

They undressed quickly, and after rolling on a condom, he slid into her. They came together as one, each giving and taking. A bone-deep warmth filled him. Jesus, he couldn't even begin to describe what she made him feel. He pumped into her and soon their cries of pleasure mingled, everything in the way they touched each other deeply intimate. As he depleted himself in her, his heart raced and he knew what had started as a stupid bet had grown into something much deeper. Jesus, he needed to call off this bet with Luke. He knew he'd be losing the one thing that meant the world to him, to Jonny. But it also meant winning the girl that had eased her way into his heart, and showed him how to live again. As he warmed to the idea, he thought about his friend, and knew in his heart that's what he would have wanted Noah to do.

* * *

For the rest of the summer, nothing seemed to matter. Nothing but Noah, painting, making love and having fun.

In a few short months he'd flipped her world upside down. It felt like freefalling without a safety net. She was completely and utterly lost in him, addicted to him. His every touch was overwhelming, his lovemaking all-consuming. The passion between them was as hot and explosive as the summer sun, and she could hardly believe how she'd gotten to this amazing place with such an incredible guy.

As she lay beside him in her bed now, their time together winding down, she thought about the future. What would happen between them when she went back to school? But thinking about school made her realize just how much she dreaded going back to her business degree.

"Noah." She turned to him and ran her fingers over his chest, reveling in the feel of his body, and loving that he wanted to be touched by her.

He put one arm under his head, and trailed his fingers over her hand. "Yeah, baby."

"I need to talk to my father."

He sat up straighter in the bed. "I know."

"I can't do this anymore. After this summer, I can't live his life. I have to start living my own. I don't want to go to business school."

Just then a knock sounded on her door. She glanced at her clock, realizing they still had ten minutes left to their lunch break.

She climbed from her bed, and smoothed down her work clothes. Noah didn't bother to move when she pulled the door open, but the second she spotted her father on the other side, her stomach jumped into her throat.

"Dad…what's…what's going on?" she asked, stumbling over her words.

An angered look moved over his face as he glanced past her shoulders to see Noah in her bed. "I think I should be the one asking that question."

"I…we…"

"So this is the reason you don't answer my calls anymore?"

"I was going to call you today," she said feebly, hearing Noah rustling behind her.

He came up beside her and held his hand out. "I'm Noah," he said introducing himself to her father.

Her father looked at Noah's work clothes, then back at Kathryn. Anger turned to disappointment, and it cut Kathryn like a knife. "Pack your bags, Kathryn. You've been here long enough to fulfill your scholarship requirements, but now I believe it's time to leave."

"No." She stood firm. "I'm not leaving."

"Kathryn," he warned. "It's clear that this wasn't the best placement for you this summer."

"Yes, it was. I learned so much about myself this summer."

Ignoring her, he said, "Next year you'll take an internship in my office."

"No, Dad, please listen."

He folded his arms, and when Noah put his hand on her shoulder for moral support, her father glared at him.

She reached her hand up and laid it over Noah's, a united force. "I don't want to work for your firm. I don't want a business degree."

"What are you talking about?"

"I want to paint. I want to be a muralist. I even got a job when I was here, and Noah—"

"And Noah's responsible for all this I take it." He looked at Noah, his gaze moving over his green resort shirt with a mixture of disdain and disapproval. "What do you do Noah?"

"I work here."

"What do you *do* here?"

"I'm a ski instructor, and white water rafting guide."

"And someone with those types of life's ambition knows what's best for my Kathryn?"

Anger moved through Kathryn as he insulted Noah. "Stop it," she said.

"No it's okay, Kat," Noah said. He stared at her father. "He's right. Maybe I don't know, but maybe your daughter does. Why don't you listen to what she has to say?"

Her father turned to her and she said, "I don't want to go back to business school."

"You'll lose your scholarship."

"Maybe they'll let me change disciplines."

"Kathryn, you have no idea what you're doing."

"Maybe, maybe not," she said, her voice strong and firm.

"You're making reckless choices."

"Maybe I am, but they're my choices." She pressed her hand to her chest, her calm slipping. "Don't you see, Dad? After Mom died, I wanted nothing more than to please you. I wanted to make you happy, to see you smile again. But the more you smiled, the less I did. I wanted to try to live the life you wanted me to, I really did." She held her arms out, laying her soul on the line. "But I was—am— miserable, completely and utterly miserable inside. You were so focused on me coming to work with you, that you didn't see it."

He jerked back and looked at her like she'd just slapped him across the face. Deep sadness moved into his eyes, and for a minute he looked like he was a million miles away. Looking lost, hurt, and deeply, deeply pained he turned from her, and without saying a word, he walked away.

Kathryn stood there, the look on his face tearing her up inside. Her eyes filled with water. She'd never meant to hurt him. She'd only wanted him to see her for who she was. "Oh, God, Noah, what have I done?"

He put his arms around her and drew her into him. She pressed her face into his chest as he stroked her hair. "Maybe he just needs time to deal with this."

Her body began to tremble, her throat so tight it was difficult to speak. "I have to go after him. I have to make this right."

"I think you both need time to cool down. You're in no shape to talk to him right now."

"I didn't mean to hurt him." Noah wiped the tears from her face. "Did you see how sad he was? Oh, God, Noah, I feel so bad."

"Come on, sit down for a minute. I'll get you a drink

of water."

He guided her to the bed and disappeared into the bathroom. As she listened to the water run, fear invaded her gut, and she knew she had to go after him. She bolted from the room, tears blurring her vision as she raced to the main lodge.

She rushed inside and frantically glanced around, trying to figure out where her father could have gone.

"Kat," Noah called out, pushing through the front doors.

Amy looked at her from behind the counter, concern in her eyes as Jared came from his office to see what all the commotion was about.

Noah caught up to her. "Kat, come on. You need to calm down."

Just then a guy Kat didn't recognize came through the front doors behind Noah.

"Well, well," he said grinning. "What do we have here?"

Noah held his hand out. "Luke, back the fuck off. Now's not the time for this."

The commotion drew both Shannon and Donald from their respective offices. Shannon had a strained smile on her face, and Donald glared at Noah like whatever was going on was his fault.

"And here I thought it was the perfect time for this," Luke responded.

"What's going on?" Kathryn asked, her glance going from Noah to Luke and back to Noah again. She spotted Jared talking to Amy at the front counter, and when she saw the look of horror on Amy's face a very bad feeling blossomed inside her.

Luke held his keys out and dangled them. "Looks like you're the proud owner of a Porsche, after all."

"I don't want your car," Noah bit out. "Just back the fuck off Luke and we'll talk about this later."

"Talk about what later?" Kathryn asked, but they both ignored her.

"Come on, you know you want it. You won it fair and square. Besides, that car's a piece of shit, and I wanted a new one anyway."

Kathryn had no idea what was going on. "You won his Porsche?"

"No," Noah said.

Luke laughed. "He sure did."

"What's going on Noah? How did you win his Porsche?"

Noah stepped between her and Luke, his voice low, dangerous when he said, "It's not what you think, Luke."

"Sure it is. I can tell by looking at her. She's far from the same all-work-and-no-play girl that came here a few months ago." He laughed. "I told you, one summer banging you, and she'd come out the other end just as fucked up." He turned to Kathryn. "You were nothing but a bet, sweetheart."

"Why are you doing this?" Noah growled.

"Because I never liked you. Because you think you can have any girl you want. Well guess what, it doesn't look like you can anymore." Luke looked over Noah's shoulders at Kathryn. "Looks like your little Kat is about to stop purring for you."

"You fucking bastard. You set this all up on purpose, just to fuck me over."

Looking cocky, Luke said, "Actually, I think it was your idea."

Before anyone could stop it, Noah drew back and slammed his fist in Luke's face. Kathryn shrieked and Donald came running over, putting himself between Noah and Luke.

"That's it, Noah," Donald said. "That's the last straw. Pack your bags. You're out of here."

Kathryn backed up, her hand covering her mouth.

She needed to run, to get as far away as possible from Noah as her entire world crashed down on her.

"Kat, wait," Noah said. He made a move toward her but Donald grabbed him by the arm. He shoved Donald off and cupped his hands around her shoulders.

She looked up at him, tears burning her eyes. "Noah, is this true?" she asked, her voice as shaky as her hands.

"Of course it's true," Luke said as he climbed from the floor, rubbing his jaw. "If he could get you in his bed, he won my car."

"Noah, please tell me it's not true," she said hysteria rising inside her.

"Just let me explain."

His words, or lack thereof, slammed through her like a physical blow. "Oh God, it is true." She pulled away from him and hugged herself. "So that's why you went after me. I was nothing but a bet." She ran her hands through her hair, pushing it from her face as tears spilled down her cheeks. "I should have known. Guys like you don't go for girls like me."

"Kat, you've got it all wrong. Please let me explain."

She swallowed hard. "So tell me, was having sex with me in the Porsche some kind of twisted victory for you?"

"Don't say that." He gave a hard shake of his head. "It was never just sex with you," he said, his voice thick with emotions. "You know that. Tell me you know that, Kat."

"I don't know anything anymore." Humiliation moved through her to think she'd been ready to throw it all away because she thought Noah believed in her. But she was nothing to him but a bet. Christ, wasn't losing her virginity…her heart…in one summer enough. Now she stood to lose her father, her job, her scholarship. Everything.

When she saw all eyes on here, including her

father's, her stomach roiled. She clasped her hand over her mouth. "I'm going to be sick."

Shannon frowned. "Kathryn, in my office now."

Kathryn pushed past her, and bolted toward the main door, unable to fight back the stinging tears.

"Pack your bags, Kathryn," her father called after her.

"Kat, wait. Don't do it. You might hate me, but you can't go back to that life, pretending to be something you're not."

She spun around, and glared at him. "You're one to talk. You of all people have no right to talk to me about pretending. Just take a look at yourself, Noah," she spat out. "Look at what you've become. You're the last person who should be lecturing me on pretending."

Haunted eyes met hers. "You're right."

"Yeah, I am right," she said. "And stay out of my life. I don't ever want to see you again." As she pushed through the door, she took one last glimpse over her shoulder and caught Noah walking toward her father.

She rushed outside and hurried to her room. She grabbed her suitcase and started throwing her clothes in it, having no idea what to do next.

"Kat," a quiet voice said at her door.

The second she set sights on Amy, she burst into tears. She dropped onto her mattress, bawling like a baby.

"Hey," Amy said, sitting on the bed next to her. "It's going to be okay."

"No, it's not."

"I'm so sorry. I didn't know. Jared never said a thing."

"So he knew, too? How humiliating."

"Yeah," she said quietly. She patted Kat's back and said, "It was a real shitty thing for Noah to do."

"Oh, yeah," she agreed, reaching for a tissue. She

blew her nose, her heart aching so badly that her body physically hurt.

"I'm guessing it's not something he'd do now, though."

"What are you talking about?"

"He's not the same guy he was a few months ago."

"Don't defend what he did, Amy."

"Oh, I'm not. Believe me, I'm not. I plan to give Jared a good reaming when he gets off tonight."

"Aren't you supposed to be at work right now, too?"

She shrugged. "You needed me." She went quiet for a moment. "So you really told your father that you didn't want to go back to business school?"

"Yeah." She held her stomach. "I feel so bad for hurting him."

"I know, but sometimes we have to stand up to our folks and prove we're adults who can make our own decisions. That took courage, Kat." A long pause and then, "I guess you're not the same girl from a few months ago either."

"What are you getting at?"

"I think you and Noah changed each other."

"I was a bet!" she cried out.

"I know, and it was shitty, but I've watched you two over the summer. It might have started as a bet for him, but I don't think it ended as one."

Kat jumped up, her emotions in a confused mess as she tossed more clothes into her suitcase.

"Are you going back?" Amy asked.

"I don't know." She turned to her friend. "I just need to be alone for a little bit."

"Okay." Amy gave her a hug and left her room.

Kat sat on her bed for what seemed like hours, thinking about what Amy had said. She stood up and paced the floor. She stopped, looked out her window and, feeling claustrophobic in her small room, headed outside. She walked aimlessly, not really knowing or caring where she was going, and was surprised to eventually find herself at the winter maintenance shed where her mural was just about finished. She used the key Noah had given her and let herself in. Heart heavy, she walked down the long hall, and stood before her mural.

She thought about her father, about Noah, about how much of a mess her life was in and started crying all over again.

"Kathryn."

Shocked, she grasped her chest and spun around to find her father standing there.

"What…how…?"

"Noah," he said. "He brought me here earlier, to show me how talented you were." He looked at the mural and Kat saw something in his face she'd never seen before. Regret. When he returned his attention to her again, he seemed older, tired. "We had a long talk."

Her heart turned over in her chest. "I don't want to talk about him."

Her father walked up to her and she rested her head on his chest as he hugged her. When she caught his warm familiar scent the tears fell harder. "I'm sorry, Dad. I said hurtful things."

"No, Kathryn. I'm the one who should be sorry."

She lifted her head and sniffed. "What?"

He exhaled slowly. "After losing you mother I was so worried about losing you too, that I hung on too tight. All I could think about was having you come to work for me. That way I could see you every day, keep you close, keep you protected. Keep you as my little girl. But I smothered you, instead." He looked past her shoulder. "I didn't let you blossom the way you needed to. I see that now."

"Daddy," she said, the tears spilling hard. "I'll always

be your little girl."

"I love you, Kathryn. I want you to be happy. If this is what makes you happy, then we need to get you switched out of business school."

She hugged him tighter. "Really?"

"Yes, really. And if the scholarship committee doesn't like it, too bad."

"Thank you."

"You can thank Noah."

She shook her head against his chest. "I don't ever want to see him again."

Her father inched back. "I don't think you can do that."

"Why?"

He turned her toward her mural. "Because every time you do something like this, you're going to remember him, remember what he did for you." She turned back toward him and he cupped her face. "Believe me I'm not very happy with what I overheard, but when I look at this, I can't help but think you need to talk to him, that there was more going on than a bet."

"I…I don't even know where to find him."

"I'm sure you do." He turned her and pointed her toward the hallway that led to the door. "Now, go before he takes off out of here."

As she walked toward the door, her mind raced with this shocking turn of events. She thought about what Amy had said, what her father had said, and all the days and nights she had spent with Noah. She thought about the times he'd come to her rescue, all the times they'd laughed, had fun, had soft and easy, or hard and fast sex well into the early hours of the morning. She thought about the way he touched her, looked at her.

She thought about the way he'd loved her.

Oh, God, what if she was too late? Donald had fired him and she'd told him she never wanted to see him again. What if he was already gone?

She ran back toward her lodge, and burst through the garage doors to find Noah revving Jonny's bike, the Porsche beside him a painful reminder of how things started between them.

"Noah," she said, breathless. "Where are you going?"

He turned the bike off and pulled off his helmet. "I'm leaving."

Her pulse leapt. "Leaving? Where are you going?"

"Back to see my family and then back to the East Coast…to school."

With her emotions in a mess, she struggled for the right words, to tell him how she felt. "I know I told you I never wanted to ever see you again and to stay out of my life…but—"

"Kat," he said interrupting her.

"Yeah?"

"I wasn't going to just leave."

"No?"

"No. I was going to find you first."

Her heart missed a beat. "You were?"

"Yeah."

"Why?"

"Because I'm not leaving here without you."

Tears welled up in her eyes. He climbed off the bike and pulled her to him. "You might hate me, Kat, and I don't blame you, but know this. I'm going to fight for you. I'm never going to stop. I'm not going to lose you." He went quiet and then placed one hand on her cheek. "I can't lose you."

"Noah," she choked out. "You…you really hurt me. I trusted you."

"I know." His eyes, a sea of stormy blue, met hers. "I'm an asshole. We already established that, remember?"

"Noah," she whispered, remembering all the fun

times they'd had.

His frowned deepened. "I can't even begin to tell you how sorry I am." He stepped closer and she could feel the heat of his body reaching out to her. "I took the bet. It was a prick thing to do and I never should have done it. I never meant to hurt you and when I really got to know you, I wanted to end the bet." He poked his thumb into his chest. "I'm not that guy anymore, Kat. You've changed me, for the better."

She nodded, understanding exactly what he was saying. She never would have stood up to her father if it hadn't been for him. "You've changed me, too."

Oh, God, she loved him so much that it hurt.

"I'm in love with you, Kat. And because of you, I'm ready to go back to school, to go back to living."

"Noah," she said, her heart softening. "I'm in love with you, too. Because of you I'm ready to live the life I've always wanted."

He exhaled. "I promise I won't ever do anything to hurt you again."

"I know."

"I talked to your father."

"I know. So did I."

"And?"

"I think everything's going to be okay."

He stared at her for a long time, his glance moving over her tear-stained face, and then he finally broke the quiet. "You know, you once told me you and your dad only had each other. But you were wrong." He opened his arms. "You've got me. That is, if you'll have me, flaws and all."

She met his eyes, everything inside her reaching out to him. "I'll have you."

She wasn't sure who moved first. The next thing she knew they were in each other's arms. As he held her, touched her, kissed her deeply, she knew that as long as they had each other, everything was going to be okay.

He inched back, and handed her a helmet. "Come on."

"Where are we going?"

He grinned and said, "To run over every last demon."

Her heart soared with the love she felt for him. "Good idea."

He planted another warm kiss onto her mouth. "Then we're going to find that happy medium we once talked about." He patted the bike seat. "But first we're going somewhere quiet because I really, really need to be inside you again.

THANK YOU!

Thank you so much for reading, Crashing Down. I hope you enjoyed Noah and Kathryn's journey as much as I loved writing it. Please read on, I've included an excerpt from Hands On with the CEO! I hope you enjoy!

Interested in leaving a review? Please do! Reviews help readers connect with books that work for them. I appreciate all reviews, whether positive or negative.

Happy Reading,
Cathryn

Coming Soon from Cathryn Fox

Like what you just read?

Be sure to like our Facebook page to find out about other Summer Lovin' releases from some of the hottest names in New Adult romance.
https://www.facebook.com/SummerLovinNewAdultRomance

Coming July 21st, Losing It, Audra North

With a childhood full of broken promises and uncertainty, forgiveness doesn't come easy for Emery Phillips. Now, with her family home on the brink of foreclosure, it's up to her to track down the elusive Theodore Chambers, Jr. and convince him to sign the clause that will extend the loan. Armed with nothing but a name and a possible location, Emery heads to Canada and Stone Cliff Resort, where she meets Ryan, a man who seems as lost as the one she seeks. An accidental encounter of *who's that sleeping in my bed* turns into a night of the hottest sex Emery has ever known. As they search for the answer to her family's future, a summer of stolen kisses and steamy passion slowly turns into much more and the fragile bond of trust begin to grow.

After a year of grieving, all Ryan Miller wants is to get his late mother's estate squared away and prepare for medical school, but even the best laid plans have a way of veering off track. First, there's the cryptic words from his mom, *I should have told you...things you need to know*. Then there's the key he found amongst her things. And finally, there's Emery, who stumbles into his room, rocks his world and, over the summer, proceeds to steal his heart. When the key unlocks the mystery of Ryan's past, will it mean a happy future for him and Emery? Or will they end up losing it all?

Coming August 4th, Loving Lies, Renee Field

Blake Samson is a man driven to succeed. Having grown up with a disinherited, alcoholic father, he knows the value of money and isn't afraid to work for it. Now, with a degree in business, he's out to prove himself to his wealthy grandfather. Securing his first major deal by acquiring Stone Cliff Resort at a rock bottom price will confirm that he's a wheeler-dealer type who won't take no for an answer, just like the old man. To accomplish his goals, Blake has put his personal life on hold, determined to remain focused on the prize, until the sexy little Gothed-up bartender dumps a drink in his lap.

Having a wealthy, Greek tycoon for a father wasn't easy for Alyssa Papadopoulos, especially one who still believed in the archaic tradition of arranged marriages to seal a business deal. Now, three years after skipping out on the groom, she'd been on her own, coping in the real world with a new name, a new look and fake history that guaranteed no one would associate her with her father. Accepting a job at Stone Cliff Resort in Alberta provides her with a good income and the opportunity to work on her one true love—photography. Getting involved with a rich bad boy didn't factor into the plan. Too bad she hasn't dated in months, and Mr. McDreamy of the lake has dimples to die for and a body that makes her hormones stand up and scream, *Oh, hell yes!*

Alyssa tries to avoid Blake, but he's determined they enjoy some summer loving, offering her a deal filled with stolen kisses and hot steamy nights she finds impossible to resist. When Blake's father dies and the world he's struggled to build begins to crumble, will Alyssa reveal the truth she so desperately holds on to, or will two people lying about their past give themselves permission to love.

Coming August 18th, Taming Tess, Jan Meredith

Once, Tess O'Neil had it all: head cheerleader, dating the most popular guy in school, a GPA of 4.0 that promised the spot of Valedictorian and a SAT score that guaranteed a full scholarship to the exclusive Culinary Arts Institute of her dreams in Nashville. Prom night was the icing on the cake…or so she thought. A date rape shatters her trust, leaving Tess skittish of a man's touch, and fearing she may never be able to have a normal relationship again. Now, three years later, she's ready to move on. When the opportunity to spend the summer at a posh vacation resort in Canada interning as a pastry chef arises, Tess welcomes the chance to get away from the past and her overprotective family. What she didn't expect was to meet a former soldier with a wounded soul and a gentle touch that awakens the woman within.

Jackson (Jax) Warren has seen enough of blood and sand. Two tours of duty in Afghanistan has left him with grit in his heart and memories that haunt his dreams. A month out of uniform with his loving but hovering family has him ready to fly apart like the IED that killed his best friend. When a fellow veteran invites him to Alberta for the summer, it's just what Jax needs. He finds solace in running Stone Cliff Resort's stables and caring for a horse in need of a gentle hand. At last he finds a modicum of piece—until a diminutive blond with big green eyes full of longing and doubt walks in to his stables. Suddenly, Jax finds himself walking a line more fragile than the minefields in the Middle East. In her arms, he finds the sleep of a peaceful heart—but when the demons come to him in the night will she still want the man they leave behind?

Coming September 1st, Surviving Nikki, Lilly Cain

Nikki Martin comes from Compton, one of the roughest neighborhoods in Toronto. She caught a break getting into the U of T, but like everything else, she's had to bust her ass to stay there, especially when there's no support from home to help pay for her degree. When her bursary becomes defunct she's desperate to find work for the summer, even if it means she has to lie on her application to score a job at a resort far from home. Hell, that might be the best part. A summer in the mountains has to be better than bumming around the city. She can figure the whole mountaineering thing out before anyone realizes she's never so much as climbed a tree—It can't be as hard as surviving in the inner city.

Evan Cade has worked at Stone Cliff Resort as a guide since he was sixteen and loves it to the point where someday he intends to buy the place, or build one just like it. So when a hotshot girl from Toronto is hired on to run one of the survival camps, he decides to take her for a test run and make sure she's as good as she claims—before some innocent camper pays the price. Out on the mountain he discovers Nikki is nothing like she reads on paper, and while some of that is good, very good, it's bad news for the camp. It's either teach her everything he knows, or cancel half the bookings and risk closing the program. He just has to get past his reaction to her and concentrate on the job at hand.

Evan has his mind on business but Nikki doesn't take direction well. Following Evan and trusting him goes against her nature. But this isn't the city and she needs the job. She can only imagine there is one thing he could want in exchange for the lessons, even if he doesn't spell it out. Nikki needs this job to survive, but can Evan really imagine surviving Nikki?

Coming September 15th,
Saving Sullivan, Sara Hubbard

Sullivan Hope is a total screw up. He finished university with the help of his father's donations to the school and an ultimatum: Straighten up and join him in the family business, or screw up again and he's cut off for good. This summer is his last chance to live it up before walking the straight and narrow in the fall, and the lure of a good party and, even better, alcohol is more than he can resist. Besides, he's never met a situation he can't handle or talk his way out of, or a pair of panties he couldn't talk his way into. That is, until he meets Abby, the nursing student full of sarcasm and sass.

Flying half way across the country to do her practical nursing placement at Stone Cliff Resort hadn't been part of Abby Claire's plans for the summer. When her first appointment, which would allow her to stay at home and care for her family, falls through, it's either pack up and go or risk not graduating. Meeting the rich, God's gift to all things on earth playboy, Sullivan Hope wasn't in her plans, either, but the more she's around him, the clearer she sees the man who hides behind the parties and liquor.

When a summer fling turns into more than either of them had bargained for, Sullivan's world begins to crumble and Abby gets dragged down into the rubble. He can't let her in despite her healing touch. And Abby can't risk getting too close and finding a reason to stay and save Sullivan.

Discover other titles by Cathryn Fox at:

www.cathrynfox.com

And be sure to sign up for her newsletter:
http://bit.ly/1kpQOzf

HANDS ON WITH THE CEO: Excerpt
New Adult Romance
Copyright 2014 by Cathryn Fox
ISBN-13: 978-0-9918032-8-6

Chapter One

Alexis Cassidy stood inside the grand villa overlooking the breathtaking Mediterranean Sea and tried to keep her jaw from dropping. She hadn't flown halfway across the country, to babysit for some rich CEO in Athens, only to come across looking like a corn-fed Iowa farm girl—one whose idea of luxurious living involved late night pizza delivery. And to think this beautiful seaside mansion was merely her employer's summer home. Heck, maybe she should forget about finishing her English degree and get involved in the software industry instead.

"Alexis," Mr. Georgiou greeted, a dazzling smile on his boyish face as he stepped farther into the airy entranceway.

"Mr. Georgiou," she responded in return, working to keep an air of professionalism about her, a difficult task considering the sudden jolt of sexual awareness turning her scholarly brain to mush. Chatting with her new employer and his four-year-old daughter over Skype was one thing, but seeing her new boss in the flesh was quite another. Not only was he smoking hot, he had an air of badness about him. Everything from his dark, sexy eyes, the rebellious length of his hair, to the confident way he moved had lust exploding inside her. As her body registered every delicious inch of him—and from the bulge in his jeans, he clearly had many delicious inches—she blew a long strand of hair off her face and shifted her purse to conceal the telltale hardening of her nipples.

The soles of his shoes tapped on the marble floor as he closed the distance between them and perfect white teeth flashed against his rich olive complexion when he said, "Welcome to our summer home."

Alexis extended her arm for a shake, but Mr. Georgiou put his hands on her shoulders and kissed her on both cheeks, one of the many Greek customs she'd read about before beginning her overseas journey. He crowded her as his mouth brushed one cheek and then the other, his warm minty breath washing over her face in scintillating ways. Hyperaware of his closeness, she became very aware of just how young and athletic he was, very aware of the way her body reacted when he pressed against her, his soft lips so damn close to hers.

So damn close...

Behind her Mr. Georgiou's limousine driver placed her luggage on the marble tile floor. "Will that be all, sir?" he asked, and Alexis inched back, thankful for the distraction before she did something that could only embarrass them both, something like angle her head so his lips landed squarely on hers.

She turned to the driver and worked to regain her composure; pretending her boss's close proximity and feel of his lips brushing her cheeks hadn't turned her knees to rubber or warmed her in all the wrong places. Exhaling slowly, she reached for her purse to give the driver a tip.

"I've got this, Alexis," Mr. Georgiou said in a thick Greek accent that sent little shivers skittering up her spine. He pulled out his wallet and stepped past her, the warm sandalwood scent of his skin curling her toes and teasing all her senses as it enveloped her. The muscles on his forearms bunched beneath the rolled up sleeves of his light blue dress shirt and it was all Alexis could do not to drool.

The man was a freaking Greek God!

She knew he was young and good looking when she'd Skyped with him a few weeks back, but the distorted image on her tablet didn't do the man justice. She also knew his multimillion-dollar software company had landed him and his partner on *Forbes'* "30 under 30" list. The man was smart, successful, driven.

Single.

Of course he hadn't always been single, but after losing the love of his life during the birth of their daughter four years ago, he'd become reclusive for a time, removing himself from the public's eyes. He reappeared as—according to the rag mags—one of Europe's richest, most eligible bachelors. Photos of him filled the tabloids, a different woman on his arm in every shot. Rumors of relationships were immediately shot down, the captions always reading the same: *according to a close personal friend, Mr. Georgiou and his current companion deny rumors of commitment…*

Alexis liked his way of thinking. She wasn't in the market for a full-time partner, either. Nor was she looking for love. She simply wanted a man to help her get in touch with her sexual self, and to teach her a thing or two in the bedroom. She cringed as she thought about the one and only guy she slept with at last year's football party. She was pretty sure he was simply giving the chubby girl a pity fuck, and when it was over, College Boy walked away and told his buddies she wasn't just fat, she was frigid.

The whole experience had been horrible and embarrassing. Not only had the reputation clung like a sweaty sports sock, following her around her entire first year of college, it was the last football party she'd been invited to. Which was why she planned to go on a strict diet for the next two months, learn her way around the bedroom, and return home a new woman. Then she'd show them!

Her glance moved over Mr. Georgiou, taking pleasure in the self-assured way he moved. He certainly looked like the guy who could give her what she needed, but he was her boss, which meant he was completely off limits. Still, she couldn't wait to text Melanie back home and tell her all about him.

As Mr. Georgiou spoke with his driver, Alexis stifled a yawn and waved to the little girl with the big brown eyes and thick dark hair as she ran into the foyer and latched on to her father's leg. Sophie waved back, and then Alexis put her hands over her face to play peek-a-boo. With two younger brothers, and having spent her high school years babysitting for nearly every family on her block, Alexis was used to being around kids. Which was why, when the ad for an *au pair* went up on the bulletin board outside the student employment center at her college—an *au pair* who majored in English and could help Mr. Georgiou's daughter refine her speech— she'd jumped all over it.

The benefits of taking the job were twofold. Not only did she need the money, which turned out to be a substantial sum, but rumor had it the men in Greece liked their women plump. With any luck she'd meet a hot guy during her time off from the job, gain a little more experience and learn to loosen up in the bedroom department before her upcoming sophomore year. A shiver moved through her. She never wanted to be called frigid again!

With the driver gone, her new boss turned back to her. "Alexis, it's so finally nice to meet you in person," he said, taking her right hand between his palms. "I'm sure you must be exhausted after travelling all day."

"I'm a little tired," she admitted. Actually she was exhausted. She'd gotten up at the crack of dawn, only to discover her flight had been delayed. She'd sat at the airport for hours, forcing herself to stay awake for fear of losing her luggage, and hadn't touched down in Greece until late this evening.

The sound of footsteps heralded someone's approach. She glanced past Mr. Georgiou to see an elderly gentleman enter the grand entranceway and collect her luggage. Dressed in formal wear, she took him to be the butler. Even though everything about the place, from the limo driver to the butler, seemed so formal, Mr. Georgiou himself appeared a little more laid back, a little easier going.

After Mr. Georgiou introduced her to the tall man with the graying hair he looked at her and said, "Damien has your room all ready for you. I'm sure you'll like it. It has one of the best views in the house." When she gave him a thankful smile, his handsome face softened, making him look even more boyish, like he could be any one of the guys sitting next to her in lecture hall. "You should try to get some sleep. Tomorrow we can go over the details of your duties."

"Okay," she agreed when Damien moved to the foot of the grand staircase.

Mr. Georgiou's voice dropped an octave, and sounded highly suggestive when he said, "And Alexis, if you need anything, anything at all, don't hesitate to ask."

Anything at all...

Alexis swallowed, heat zinging through her blood as she considered the provocative edge to his voice. When she stole another glance at him, he gave her a polite smile, nothing on his attractive face to suggest he'd been hinting at something more intimate.

She shook her head to clear it, sure her jet-lagged mind was simply playing tricks on her.

His hand cut through the air. "Our home is your home and we want you to be comfortable here."

"Thank you," she said, relaxing as she once again took in the opulence of the place.

"But before you go…" Mr. Georgiou put his hands on his daughter's shoulders and moved her in front of him. "I'd like you to meet Sophie. Sophie, you remember Skyping with Alexis don't you?"

Sophie nodded, peeking up at Alexis shyly as she curled her ponytail around her finger.

"Hi, Sophie," Alexis said, then crinkled her nose, and looked up the huge staircase. Hoping to put the child at ease by enlisting her help and assigning her responsibilities, she said, "I'm glad you're here to help me out and show me around. Otherwise I might get lost in this place."

Sophie stopped playing with her hair, and stood a little taller, clearly liking the idea of being in charge. "I won't let you get lost," she said, a childish confidence to her voice.

"I knew I could count on you." She held her hand out to the little girl, and nodded toward the wide staircase. "Do you think maybe you can help me find my room?" From her previous exchanges with Mr. Georgiou, she knew how much the girl loved the ocean, so she added, "If I get lost in the hall for days, I'll never be able to take you to the beach tomorrow."

Sophie giggled and when she stepped forward and accepted Alexis's hand, Mr. Georgiou smiled. "I can already see Sophie is in good hands."

Her glance went to his chin, to where he was scrubbing his palm over his five o'clock shadow.

Speaking of good hands…

Shaking off a shiver, she let Sophie lead her to the stairs, but stopped when Mr. Georgiou said, "Oh, and Alexis, one more thing." She turned and when dark, sexy eyes locked on hers, heat moved through her body. She swallowed the little rush bubbling in her throat and opened her mouth to speak, but before she could find her words, he said, "Call me Nikko."

"Okay," she managed to push out. "I'll see you in the morning, Nikko." She turned her attention to the massive staircase, hoping her knees wouldn't fail her as she climbed. She gripped the handrail, and held tight as she made her way up.

She chattered with Sophie as the little girl showed her to her lavish room. Once Damien delivered her luggage, he shooed Sophie out so Alexis could have some privacy while getting settled in. After the two disappeared, she spread her arms wide and couldn't keep the smile from her face. She took it the king-sized mattress, pretty floral bedding, gorgeous furniture and the *en suite* bathroom that was hers and hers alone. A little squeal sounded in her throat as she reveled in her good fortune. She grabbed her phone from her bag, punched in Melanie's number and walked to the elaborate, floor-to-ceiling window with a spectacular view of the moonlit ocean. She pushed back the sheer curtain, released the latch on the window to push them open, and breathed in the salty sea air. A warm breeze rushed inside and ruffled her lacy curtains.

"Oh. My. God," she whispered when she spotted the infinity pool overlooking the ocean. She could just imagine herself lounging beside that pool, sipping a fruity drink and staring out at the view.

"Oh. My. God. What?" Melanie asked, concern in her voice.

She shrieked when she heard her friend. "Mel, you wouldn't believe this place."

"Oh Jesus, you scared the living shit out of me," she scolded. Then she gave a loud sigh and said, "I knew it would be awesome."

"Awesome doesn't even begin to describe it."

"Tell me everything," Mel demanded, and Alexis

could just picture her friend throwing herself on her bed, pissed off that she was stuck at home working the corn fields instead of taking her own *au pair* job like she wanted. "If I can't be there, then you at least have to let me live vicariously through you. So now tell me everything, and don't leave out a single detail."

Alexis shot a glance toward her closed door and lowered her voice. "Nikko is unbelievably gorgeous."

"Nikko," she sighed again. "Even his name is hot."

"Everything about him is hot."

"Wait, you're on a first name basis with him?" Mel asked.

"He insisted."

"Umm," Mel purred. "Sounds like a man who likes being in control. I wonder what else you'd do if he insisted."

Alexis laughed. "He's my boss and I want to keep this job," she said, even though she secretly wondered that herself.

"He might be your boss but not only is he young, gorgeous and a notorious playboy; he's fucking rich, Alex. Rich!"

Exactly, which was why he had numerous waif-like models throwing themselves at him and wouldn't give a plump farmer's daughter a second glance. Not that she would ever try to seduce her boss, or act on the delicious things he made her feel, but it still didn't stop her from thinking about it.

Deciding to redirect the conversation, Alexis pulled her curtain back, taking in all the other mansions dotting the mountain. "Nikko was right, the view is breathtak..." Her voice trailed off, her tongue thickening at the unexpected vision before her, a vision more beautiful than the cerulean waters lapping against the sandy shoreline far below her window.

"Hello? Alex, are you still there?"

"Oh my God."

"Now what!"

"I just saw my neighbor." Patio lanterns illuminated the grounds next door, giving sufficient light for her to see the man in the scant bathing suit as he climbed onto the diving board. Her glance moved over him, trailing down the firm ridges of his abdomen, to follow the sexy line of hair that disappeared into the material that did little to hide the huge bulge her fingers suddenly itched to explore. A wheezing sound escaped her lips. Alexis squinted her eyes and focused on his torso…and the area due south. Surely it was a play of the lanterns reflecting off the water that caused all those mouthwatering ridges, bulges and dips on his body? Sort of, nature's way of Photoshopping.

She heard Mel sigh. "I take it he's hot too."

"Oh yeah. He's in a Speedo and he just dove into his pool." Alex gripped the curtain and leaned out her window for a better view. When Mr. Speedo surfaced on the other end, his hand came up to smooth his hair back and his gaze lifted to her bedroom window. A small, sensual smile touched his mouth when their gazes collided beneath the moonlight. Alexis dropped the curtain and jumped back, her heart hammering against her ribcage.

"Oh, shit. He just caught me staring." She quickly threw herself on her bed, her long dark curls splaying across her pillowcase. "How frigging embarrassing. He probably thinks I'm a voyeur." She clamped her hand over her eyes at the thought, then snorted and flung it back onto her pillow. Too late for that now.

"The hell with being embarrassed. That's fucking hot! Let him know you're looking. Let him know you're interested, that you like what you see. Isn't that what you wanted—a sexy man to notice you, to give you some experience?"

"Yes, but…"

"No buts. This is it, girl. Don't you dare puss out. Go for it!"

Alex's stomach tightened as she thought about opening the curtain again, doing exactly as Mel suggested. Instead she groaned and rolled to her side.

"I'm not like you, Mel."

"Come on, Alex. One of the reasons you took this job was to sample the local cuisine."

"I know," she groaned and rubbed her hand over her stomach where butterflies took flight at the thought of Mr. Speedo pulling her into his arms and… "but he's so incredibly hot."

"So are you."

She frowned, knowing otherwise, but instead of dwelling on her full figure, she asked, What if he's married?"

"What if he's not?"

"But he's Nikko's neighbor." What if she made a move on him and he wasn't interested in more than flirting. If he told Nikko, she'd have to live with the embarrassment for the duration of her stay. On the other hand, what if she didn't act on it, and missed out on the very thing she'd come to Greece for?

"Perfect."

Alexis ran her hand along the soft bedding. "Why is that perfect?"

"Because," she began, stretching out that one word. "if you can watch him, it means he can watch you, too."

"And what exactly will he be watching?" Alexis asked, not sure if she wanted to hear the answer.

"You, sunbathing by the pool, topless, and bending over. A lot."

Alexis laughed. "You are so bad."

"And I bet Mr. Speedo is so fucking *good*."

As a surge of heat moved through her, Alexis

climbed from the bed and inched her curtain open again. She stole another peek at her young, well-built neighbor as he lounged against the side of the pool, his arms braced on the ledge, showing off a hard body that was clearly made for sex.

Alexis gulped when he glanced her way again.

"Oh shit, he's looking at me," she whispered into the phone, her pulse leaping like mad.

"Good, now give him something to look at," Mel said.

He gave her a lopsided panty melting smile and crooked his finger.

"Oh. My. God. He's inviting me to come down."

Her friend squealed. "Jesus, Alex. Go for it."

Alexis's body flushed hotly as she pictured herself accepting his invitation, going down there in the sexy thong bathing suit Mel insisted she buy, and joining her hot neighbor in the pool like it was the most natural thing in the world for her to do.

She wet her bottom lip and asked in a low voice, "You really think I could seduce him?"

"Yes, girlfriend, I know you can seduce him. So get down there and do it!"

Acknowledgements

A book never comes together alone, and this one is no exception. I would like to give a great big thank you to Jan, Audra, Lilly, Renee and Sara for all the brainstorming sessions, and for reading every version, even those early scary one!

A huge thank you to my Mark, Alex and Allison. You all had a part in shaping this story, from the motorcycle information, the overachieving scholarship student, to the graffiti (Allison I love the M&M).

A huge thank you to my street team. You gals are the best! Thank you for your reviews and support. I appreciate you all so much!

To the people behind the scenes who made the book look good: Crocodesigns, for the gorgeous cover, Ironhorse formatting for making the pages perfect, and Debra Stang for the editing…thank you!

Cathryn

OTHER TITLES BY CATHRYN FOX

Hands On with the CEO
Yours to Take
Torn Between Two Brothers
Spring Fling
His Obsession Next Door
Flirty in Whispering Cover
Hold Me Down Hard
Holiday Spirit
Pleasure Control

**To discover even more titles by Cathryn Fox check
out her website at
www.CathrynFox.com**

ABOUT CATHRYN FOX

New York Times and *USA today* Bestselling author, Cathryn is a wife, mom, sister, daughter, and friend. She loves dogs, sunny weather, anything chocolate (she never says no to a brownie) pizza and red wine. She has two teenagers who keep her busy with their never ending activities, and a husband who is convinced he can turn her into a mixed martial arts fan. Cathryn can never find balance in her life, is always trying to find time to go to the gym, can never keep up with emails, Facebook or Twitter and tries to write page-turning books that her readers will love.

Connect with Cathryn:
Newsletter: http://bit.ly/1kpQOzf
Twitter: https://twitter.com/writercatfox
Facebook:
https://www.facebook.com/AuthorCathrynFox?ref=hl
Blog: http://cathrynfox.com/blog/
Goodreads:
https://www.goodreads.com/author/show/91799.Cathryn
_Fox
Pinterest http://www.pinterest.com/catkalen/